Love on the Fence

An Interracial Romance

Queenink Watkins

Baobab Publishing

ACKNOWLEDGEMENTS:

In all things, I give thanks to God because without Him, I would not have life nor talent.

DISCLAIMER: WORK OF FICTION

This is a work of fiction. Names, characters, places, and events are either products of the author's imagination or are used fictitiously. Any resemblance to actual persons, living or dead, or real events is purely coincidental.
The views and actions expressed by the characters do not reflect the beliefs, values, or opinions of the author.

I write realistic fiction inspired by the world around me and the ideas circulating within it—sometimes shocking, sometimes uncomfortable, but always rooted in storytelling, not personal ideology.

Reader discretion is advised.

TRIGGER WARNING

This book contains content that may be disturbing or triggering to some readers, including scenes of sexual manipulation, and racial tension. Reader discretion is advised.

DEDICATION:

To all the incredible single moms navigating this wild journey of life—I see you. This book is for the warriors hustling through financial struggles, juggling work, parenting, and a million other things. Your strength is inspirational. Remember, your value is immeasurable, and don't let anyone tell you otherwise. Keep your heart open because love has a funny way of finding us when we least expect it. Here's to your journey and to finding that "good man" who truly deserves you. You've got this! 🩶

TITLES TO LOOK FOR BY QUEENINK WATKINS:

- [ ] Perfect Love
- [ ] Open Door Policy
- [ ] Pucking With a Loser
- [ ] Envious Betrayal
- [ ] The Bride
- [ ] Perfect Lies
- [ ] Bleeding Love
- [ ] The Office Playboy
- [ ] Urban Legends
- [ ] Perfect Life
- [ ] Next Christmas

Contents

Chapter 1

A Responsible Adult

Carmen Diaz

Carmen fumbled with her keys, balancing her squirming two-year-old daughter on her hip. She took a deep breath in, then exhaled, preparing herself to go inside, as she finally managed to unlock the door to their tiny apartment.

"Home at last, mija."

As Carmen stepped inside, the scent of stale air and dirty dishes hit her nose like a braggart boxer. She shook her head at the chaos surrounding her. Toys were strewn across the faded linoleum in the breakfast area. In the kitchen, clothes hung haphazardly over bar stool backs, and dishes piled high in the sink.

"Messy, Mama."

"Yes, baby. It's messy." She thought to herself, 'I can't believe he left it like this. Again.' Carmen's long bleach blonde hair fell in her face as she bent to put Mia down.

The sound of rapid gunfire and explosions suddenly erupted from the living room, making Carmen flinch. She peered around the corner to see Tony on the couch with his eyes glued to the TV screen, frantically mashing buttons on the game controller.

"Tony," Carmen called out. No response. "Tony!" she repeated, louder this time.

He barely glanced up. "Oh, hey babe. You're home." His attention immediately returned to the game.

Carmen walked over, purposely blocking his view of the screen. "Have you been playing all day?"

Tony leaned to the side, trying to see past her. "Just a few hours. No big deal."

'A few hours? More like all day, judging by the mess.' The smell of stale snacks and sweat were pungent indicators of the hours he'd truly spent locked away from reality. His black hair was wild, falling all over his forehead and he still hadn't shaved. He was beginning to look and smell like a werewolf. She couldn't take it anymore, but she was trying her best to hang on, to make this family thing work for her daughter's sake. Carmen began removing Mia's coat. She walked back over to the foyer to hang it on the leaning rack by the door.

"So, what's for dinner?" Tony asked, his eyes never leaving the screen. "I'm starving."

Carmen froze with her hand still on Mia's jacket. 'He expects me to cook after all this?' She took a deep breath, trying to keep her voice level. "I just got home, Tony. I haven't even had a chance to think about dinner."

"Well, can you whip something up? I've worked up an appetite."

'Worked up an appetite doing what? Playing games all day while I bust my ass at work?' She bit her tongue, not wanting to argue in front of Mia. "I'll see what I can do."

"Mommy, potty!"

"Okay, sweetie, let's go." As Carmen grabbed Mia's hand and hurried towards the bathroom, a thought stopped her. "Tony, did you pick up those overnight trainers I asked for?"

Tony's silence was deafening.

"Tony?" she called out again.

"Uh, I might've forgotten," he finally answered, his voice muffled by distance.

Carmen closed her eyes, counting to ten. She absentmindedly let go of Mia's hand and strode to the kitchen, scanning the pantry. Her frustration mounted as she noticed several other missing items.

"You forgot the trainers and half the grocery list," she said, returning to the living room. "What exactly did you do today?"

Tony paused his game, looking defensive. "I got most of it. And I had stuff to do, you know."

"Stuff? Like what? Playing games and hanging out with your buddies?"

"Hey, I work too."

Carmen scoffed. "Part-time, Tony. While I'm working full-time at the pharmacy and take care of Mia."

"I contribute," he insisted.

"Really? Because from where I'm standing, it looks like I'm carrying all the weight while you party with your friends and hit up strip clubs."

"That's not fair. I help out."

"Help out? This isn't about 'helping out'. This is about being a responsible partner and father!" Carmen was heated now. She didn't want to yell, but that's what she found herself doing.

Tony switched his game off and stood up, his voice rising to match Carmen's. "You're always nagging me about something. I can't do anything right in your eyes!"

"Nagging? Is that what you call asking you to be a responsible adult?"

As they argued, their voices grew louder. Tony's words became a cluster of excuses and deflections, each one grating on Carmen's already frayed nerves.

"You don't appreciate anything I do. I'm doing my best here!"

Carmen opened her mouth to retort, but a small whimper from the hallway caught her attention. Mia stood there, tears streaming down her face with a dark wet spot spreading across her pants.

"Oh, Mia." Carmen's anger was instantly replaced by concern.

Tony glanced at Mia, then back at Carmen. "See what you did? You upset her with all your yelling."

Carmen clenched her teeth. She wanted to scream at him, to point out his hypocrisy, but Mia's sniffles held her back. Taking a deep breath, she walked over to their daughter.

"It's okay, mija," she responded, scooping Mia into her arms. "Accidents happen. It's my fault for making you wait too long."

As she headed towards the bathroom, Carmen pressed a gentle kiss to Mia's forehead. "Shh, it's alright. Mommy's got you."

Carmen felt her anger at Tony intensify, even as she worked to keep her voice calm for Mia's sake. How dare he blame her for this? she thought. If he'd just remembered to get the things on the list...

• • • • • • • • • • •

Carmen gently lowered Mia into the warm bathwater, her daughter's tears subsiding as she played with her rubber ducky. "There we go, mi amor. All better now." Carmen smiled, washing Mia's back.

After drying and dressing Mia, Carmen carried the playpen into the living room. She then settled her daughter in it, surrounding Mia with her favorite stuffed animals. "Look, Mia. It's Dora time," Carmen said, switching on the TV. Mia's eyes lit up at the familiar theme song.

Carmen lingered a moment, watching Mia babble happily at the screen. She steeled herself before heading back to the kitchen.

There she found Tony, one hand on his stomach, peering into the open fridge. He turned as she entered. "Hey, Car. What's for dinner? I'm starving."

She couldn't believe after all that just happened that he was still bugging her about cooking. But she kept her voice level. "I just got home, Tony. I haven't had time to think about dinner."

Tony shut the fridge, frowning. "But you know I get hungry around this time. Can't you whip something up quick?"

Carmen felt her patience wearing thin. She took a deep breath, reminding herself that Mia was just in the next room. "Tony, I've been working all day. Why didn't you start dinner?"

Carmen turned to the cabinets, pulling out a pot and a box of spaghetti. She grabbed tomato sauce and ground beef from the fridge, slamming it hard. As she set the ingredients on the counter, her frustration bubbled over. Tony was already thirty. Three years older than her, but she felt like the only grown-up between them. He made her feel like she was raising two toddlers instead of one.

"You know what, Tony? I'm done. I can't do this anymore. I think you need to leave."

"What? Come on, Car. You can't be serious."

"I am," Carmen replied, turning to face him. "You barley work, you don't help with Mia, you don't even do basic chores. I'm carrying everything, and I'm exhausted."

Tony stepped closer. "Look, I know things have been tough, but we can work it out. This place is cheap, and my income helps with the rent."

Carmen scoffed. "Your part-time income barely covers groceries."

"Yeah, but you make more money," Tony argued. "If anyone should move out, it should be you. You could afford a nicer place for you and Mia."

"Are you kidding me? This is my home, Tony. I'm not uprooting my daughter because you refuse to grow up."

They went back and forth, voices rising. Carmen thought of Mia in the next room and tried to keep her tone down.

Finally, she exhaled heavily. "Fine. If that's how you want to play it, I'll look for something else. But this is bullshit, Tony."

Chapter 2

A Day in Accounting

Jamal Adams

Leaning forward in his leather chair, Jamal Adams clasped his espresso-toned hands together on his desk of organized chaos. Across from him sat Mr. Johnson, owner of a new dry cleaning business, fidgeting with his collar. The scent of starch and detergent clung to Mr. Johnson's clothes.

"So, you're saying your wife's struggling with the bookkeeping?"

"She can't add two and two without a calculator. I swear, sometimes I think she's trying to sabotage the business."

Jamal suppressed a sigh. He'd heard this story before of husbands blaming wives for financial woes.

"Let's focus on solutions," he suggested. "I can offer a comprehensive accounting package that'll take the stress off both of you."

As Jamal outlined his services, he noticed Mr. Johnson's gaze drifting. The man's fingers tapped an impatient rhythm on the armrest.

"And another thing," Mr. Johnson interrupted, "she can't even balance a checkbook. How am I supposed to trust her with our livelihood?"

Jamal was getting irritated, but he maintained his professional demeanor. He'd hoped to highlight his accounting services, but for fifteen minutes, all he'd heard were complaints about this man's incompetent wife. He thought of his father's advice: "Sometimes, son, people just need to be heard."

"I understand your frustration, Mr. Johnson," Jamal said, leaning back slightly. "But blaming won't solve the problem. What if we set up a system that's easy for both of you to use?"

"You don't get it. She's hopeless with numbers. Always has been."

Jamal glanced at the clock again. Nearly twenty minutes had passed, and they'd made little progress. He wondered if this potential client was more interested in venting than finding a solution. Still, he persevered, determined to offer guidance if Mr. Johnson would listen.

"Let's look at it this way," Jamal began, reaching for a notepad. "What if we..."

Jamal's phone buzzed, interrupting his train of thought. Dad's name flashed on the screen. Jamal answered the call considering it could be news about his mom's upcoming surgery. He told his dad to hold on a second.

"I apologize, Mr. Johnson, but our free consultation time is up," Jamal said, rising from his chair. He reached into his pocket and pulled out a business card. "Please, take this and consider our services. I believe we can help streamline your business finances."

Mr. Johnson nodded, taking the card. "Thanks for your time," he replied, clearly still preoccupied with his own grievances.

As the door closed behind his potential client, Jamal resumed the call. "Hey, Dad. Everything okay? What's the update?"

"Surgery's set for next month. Your mother's worried about work, though. That supervisor of hers..."

"That's ridiculous," Jamal replied. "They can't fire her for taking medical leave. That's a lawsuit waiting to happen."

"I hear you, son," his father responded, wearily. "But you know how these things go. They're smart enough to make up something else if they want to."

Jamal leaned back, staring at the ceiling. He was torn between wanting to reassure his father and acknowledging the harsh realities they might face. "Dad, we can't let fear stop Mom from getting the care she needs."

Jamal took a deep breath. "Look, let's not think the worst just yet. Have you heard the good news about Keyana?"

"No, what's that?"

"I spoke to her yesterday. She's decided to live off campus this coming semester," Jamal said, a smile creeping into his voice. "She'll be home to help care for Mom while you're at work. It's perfect timing, really."

"Oh, that is good news! Your sister's always had a knack for showing up when we need her most."

"That's our Keyana. Always looking out for the family."

There was a moment of comfortable silence before his father spoke again. "So, when can we expect to see you?"

Jamal's eyebrows drew together as he looked at the stack of files still waiting for him on his desk. This week's accounting project had him working late most nights. He glanced at his calendar, quickly scanning the upcoming dates. "I'll be by tonight around 7:30," he said, deciding to leave a little earlier tonight. "And I'll drop by the day before the surgery and spend some time with Mom. I'll be there right after she gets back home and settled, too. Whatever you guys need, I'm here."

"That means a lot, son. Your mother will appreciate that."

They wrapped up the call and Jamal headed to the break room, his mind heavy with concern for his mother.

A whiff of fresh coffee hit him as he pushed open the door, momentarily distracting him from his worries. Tavaris Johnson, Jamal's clean-cut tall and muscular homeboy from college was already in there when he arrived. Jamal had gotten Tavaris a job at the firm a year ago after he'd been laid off from another firm. Tavaris nudged Jamal as he entered.

"Check it out," he whispered, nodding towards Brandi Hunt.

There, leaning against the counter with a steaming mug in hand, stood Brandi. Her dark eyes locked onto Jamal's, a hint of a smile playing on her lips.

"She's been eyeing you since you walked in," Tavaris teased. "Might be your lucky day, bro."

Jamal chuckled, shaking his head. "Nah, T. That's all you."

"You serious?" Tavaris's eyebrows shot up. "Brandi's fine as hell. What's the deal?"

Jamal poured himself a cup of coffee, considering his words. "Look, she's attractive, no doubt. But that's not everything, you know?"

"What, too much woman for you?"

"She's not my type, that's all," Jamal responded, trying his best not to have to go into details as to why he wasn't into his co-worker.

"Everybody can't be Kelis, so you might as well get that out of your head."

Kelis was Jamal's ex. She was sophisticated, smart and sexy, had gorgeous bronze skin and rocked the cutest little fro. They broke up two and a half years ago when she decided to leave the clinic she worked for and become a traveling nurse. Long distance just wasn't working, at least that's what Kelis explained the night she called and ended their five-year relationship.

"It's not that," Jamal said, stirring his coffee. "She's just... I don't know. Too direct, I guess. I like a bit of mystery, a challenge."

Tavaris laughed, clapping Jamal on the shoulder. "Man, you and your challenges. Some of us appreciate a woman who knows what she wants."

Jamal smiled, his eyes drifting back to Brandi for a moment. She was undeniably beautiful, but something in him just didn't spark. "Then by all means, T. She's all yours."

Brandi set her mug down and glided across the room, in sky-high heels so slender they seemed better suited for display than walking. As she approached, Jamal noticed a subtle change in her demeanor. Her usual confident swagger was tempered, replaced by a softer, more approachable air.

"Hey guys," Brandi said, her voice warm but not overly enthusiastic. "How's the Hendrix account coming along Jamal?"

Jamal offered a polite smile. "It's moving forward. Just ironing out some details."

Tavaris spoke up. "Yeah, Jamal's a real wizard with numbers. He'll have it wrapped up in no time."

Brandi nodded, her eyes lingering on Jamal. "I'm not surprised. Your reputation precedes you, Jamal."

Jamal felt a twinge of discomfort at the compliment but kept his expression neutral. "I'm definitely not a wizard.

"So," Brandi continued, "any plans for the weekend? I heard about this new jazz club downtown."

Tavaris perked up. "Oh yeah? Sounds cool. What's it called?"

As Brandi discussed the club, Jamal found his mind wandering. He appreciated her attempt at subtlety, but the underlying intent was clear. He tuned back in just as Tavaris was readily agreeing that they should all check it out sometime.

"That'd be great," Brandi said, her smile bright. She turned to Jamal. "What do you think? You in?"

Jamal hesitated, searching for a diplomatic response. "Sounds interesting, but I've got family commitments this weekend. Maybe another time."

Clear disappointment crossed Brandi's face, quickly masked by understanding. "Of course, family first. Well, the offer stands."

As the conversation continued, Jamal found himself nodding along, offering brief responses when necessary. He couldn't help but notice how Tavaris hung on Brandi's every word, clearly captivated. For Jamal, though, the small talk only reinforced his initial impression. Brandi was lovely, but there was no spark, no intrigue that pulled him in.

As Brandi walked away, a confident smile playing on her lips, Tavaris let out a low whistle. His eyes followed her retreating figure, fixated on the sway of her hips.

"Damn, look at that *Georgia Peach* as she walks away," Tavaris drooled. "Shake it, baby, shake it."

Jamal couldn't help but glance in Brandi's direction, but his attention quickly returned to Tavaris. His friend's dramatized gestures and slack-jawed expression were far more entertaining than Brandi's exaggerated curves.

"You seem impressed," Jamal remarked dryly, raising an eyebrow at Tavaris.

Tavaris grinned, still watching Brandi disappear around the corner. "Can you blame me? That body is something else."

Jamal shifted uncomfortably, debating whether to say anything. He knew the truth - that Brandi's current figure was the result of skillful surgery rather than nature's bounty. Two years ago, there had been significantly less to admire. But Tavaris had joined the company after Brandi's transformation, blissfully unaware of her physical evolution.

"It's definitely... eye-catching," Jamal said carefully, not wanting to lie outright.

"Eye-catching? Man, that's the understatement of the year," Tavaris laughed, finally tearing his gaze away. "You know, maybe I should ask her out."

Jamal tensed, knowing Tavaris' tendency to let things slip in casual conversation. If he pursued Brandi and found out about her surgery, it would be all over the office in no time.

"You sure that's a good idea?" Jamal asked, trying to keep his tone neutral. "Office romances can get messy."

Chapter 3

The Kind Dark Stranger

Carmen Diaz

Carmen stared at the unmoving sea of cars in front of her. The sound of idling engines, punctuated by the occasional honk of frustration from the trapped commuters. She glanced in the rearview mirror at Mia, who sat contentedly in her car seat, playing with a small stuffed rabbit.

"Two hundred dollars," Carmen blurted out, shaking her head. "How am I supposed to afford that?"

The daycare's rate increase was definitely happening at the wrong time. With Tony out of the picture, her already tight budget was about to become suffocating. She raked through her bleach blonde hair with her fingers, pushing it back from her face.

"Mama, look!" Mia babbled, holding up her toy, swinging it back and forth. "Bunny fly!"

"That's great, sweetie. Bunny's having fun, huh?"

As she turned back to face the road, Carmen's smile faded. The traffic hadn't moved an inch. She was getting frustrated, already anxious over her financial situation.

"Come on, move already!"

The GPS on her phone announced that her arrival time in Newnan had been pushed back another fifteen minutes. Carmen sighed, picturing the tiny rental home waiting for them. It wasn't much, but it was a fresh start—if she could keep affording it.

"Shit! Why don't you guys go already?" she yelled, her patience snapping. Immediately, she regretted her outburst, glancing back at Mia. Thankfully, she seemed unfazed, still engrossed in her make-believe bunny adventure.

Carmen took a deep breath, trying to calm herself. "It's okay," she whispered. "We'll figure this out. We always do, right Mia?"

"Right, Mama!" Mia replied automatically, though Carmen knew she hadn't really understood the question.

The brake lights ahead finally began to dim. Just as traffic started to move, Carmen's phone lit up with

Lola's call. She tapped the steering wheel to answer, grateful for the distraction.

"Hey, cuz."

"You sound beat. Everything okay?" Lola pressed.

Carmen sighed, merging into the right lane. "They jacked up daycare rates again. Another two hundred a month."

"What? That's insane! How are you gonna manage that?"

"I don't know," Carmen admitted. "And that's not even the worst part. I've got no furniture except Mia's stuff. Been sleeping on an air mattress in a sleeping bag. It's freezing at night."

"Girl, why didn't you say something? Ask your parents for help. Maybe they could spot you for a futon or something?"

"I can't. I'm not ready to tell them about Tony. You know papá. I'd never hear the end of his 'I told you he was a loser' lecture."

"Carmen—," Lola started, but Carmen cut her off.

"I know, I know. I just... I can't deal with that right now."

They continued talking, Carmen's eyes switching between the road and her rearview mirror, where Mia sat contentedly playing with her rabbit.

Suddenly, Carmen's phone beeped with another incoming call. Her stomach dropped as she saw the name.

"Speaking of the devil," she reacted. "Lola, I gotta go. Tony's calling."

"Alright, girl. Stay strong," Lola encouraged before hanging up.

Carmen took a deep breath, steeling herself before answering. "Hello?"

"Hey, babe," Tony's voice oozed sweetness. "I've missed you this week. When are you coming home?"

Carmen rolled her eyes and shook her head. "I'm not, Tony. You know that."

"Aw, come on. Put me on speaker. Let me say hi to my little princess."

Reluctantly, Carmen complied. "Mia, say hi to Daddy."

"Hi, Daddy!" Mia squealed, her face lighting up.

As Mia babbled excitedly, Carmen felt hurt about her daughter being separated from her father. This was why leaving had been so hard. But she had to remind herself why she'd done it.

"Tony," she interrupted, "I signed a six-month lease. I'm not coming back."

"Then I'll move in with you," he suggested. "Our lease here is up in two months anyway."

"Are you kidding me?" Carmen snapped. "After everything—"

"Hey, hey," Tony's voice turned stern. "You know Mia doesn't like it when we argue."

Carmen held her anger, forcing herself to calm down. "Look, Tony. We need to talk about the day-care payment for next week. It's due tomorrow, and they've gone up fifty dollars a week."

Tony's sigh crackled through the phone. "Carmen, you know I can't help with that. I'm only working part-time."

"Then why'd you call?"

"Well...I was hoping you could help me out with groceries. You took half the food when you left, and I'm running low."

The realization hit Carmen hard. "Seriously? That's why you're being so sweet?"

"Come on, babe—"

"Don't 'babe' me!" Carmen exploded. "I can't stand your no-good ass, Tony! You're such a freakin' manipulator. Get a life!"

"Carmen, please, I'm sorry—" Tony's apologies were cut short as Carmen jabbed the end call button.

In the backseat, Mia started to whimper. Carmen glanced in the rearview mirror, catching sight of her daughter's trembling lower lip.

"It's okay, mija," Carmen soothed, shame striking her conscience. "Mommy's just tired."

As she refocused on the road, Carmen realized her exit was coming up. But her GPS was no loner giving direction. Panic grew as she realized she couldn't remember which road to take next.

"Shit!" she reacted, fumbling with her phone. She tapped the screen, trying to reactivate the GPS while stealing quick glances at the road. Hurriedly, she typed in her new address: 639 Maple Hurst Ln.

"Please work," she whispered, praying she wouldn't miss her turn or worse, cause an accident.

Carmen hadn't driven 10 minutes before her check battery light came on. The car sputtered and died, barely giving her time to pull onto the shoulder.

"No, no, no," Carmen muttered, gripping the wheel. She glanced back at Mia, relieved to see her daughter had fallen peacefully asleep. At least one thing was going right.

Carmen stepped out, the cool evening air nipping at her skin. She popped the trunk, searching for the electric jumper cables her father had gifted her. Her hands came up empty.

"Right," she sighed, slamming the trunk shut. "Tony has those too."

A cry pierced the air. Carmen winced, realizing she'd startled Mia awake. She slid into the backseat, pulling her daughter close.

"Shh, mija," she said, stroking Mia's dark curls. "Everything's okay. Mommy's here."

As Mia's breathing evened out, Carmen's mind raced. Who could she call? Lola and Felicia were too far away in Rex. She bit her lip, weighing her options.

"The insurance," she remembered suddenly. "I still have those emergency services."

Just as she reached for her phone, headlights illuminated the interior of her car. She turned to see a sleek sedan had pulled up behind her, and a well-built man with espresso skin stepped out.

Carmen's heart hammered. Help or threat? She held Mia tighter, watching warily as the stranger approached.

The man tapped lightly on her window. Carmen hesitated, then rolled it down a crack.

"You got someone coming to help, or are you out here alone?" he asked.

Carmen was afraid. The road was nearly empty and it was getting darker. She glanced at her phone: 6:40 PM.

"I... I'm waiting for roadside assistance," she lied.

The man nodded, his kind eyes crinkling at the corners. "They can take a while sometimes. Mind if I take a look?"

Carmen weighed her options. The emergency service could take forever, and Mia was getting restless. This stranger seemed genuine, but...

"It's okay if you'd rather wait," he added, sensing her hesitation. "Just thought I'd offer."

His easy demeanor and well-groomed appearance (dress coat, pointy-toe shoes, a neat box fade and trimmed beard), slowly eased Carmen's fears.

She took a deep breath. "Actually, if you wouldn't mind..."

"Not at all," he smiled, extending his hand. "I'm Jamal. Jamal Adams."

"Carmen Diaz," she replied, shaking it briefly.

As Jamal moved to the front of the car, Carmen's eyes followed him. There was something captivating about his confident movements.

"Could you pop the hood for me?" Jamal called.

Carmen obliged, watching as he examined the engine. His brow furrowed in concentration, and she found herself oddly drawn to his focused expression.

"Looks like your battery's dead," he announced. "I've got jumper cables if you'd like a jump."

"That would be amazing," Carmen said, relief washing over her. "Thank you so much."

As Jamal retrieved the cables, Carmen allowed herself a small smile. Maybe there were still good people in the world after all.

After Jamal successfully jumped her car, Carmen leaned against the driver's door, her shoulders relaxing for the first time since her breakdown.

"I can't thank you enough," she said, tucking a strand of blonde hair behind her ear. "We're new to Newnan, and I wasn't sure who to call."

Jamal's eyes lit up. "Welcome to the neighborhood! How are you liking it so far?"

"Well, we just moved in, so I'm still getting my bearings."

"It's a great town," Jamal said. "Lots of history, but plenty of modern amenities too."

Carmen nodded, trying to discern whether he was flirting. She pushed the thought away, reminding herself of her recent split with Tony.

"That's good to hear," she replied, glancing back at Mia, who was wide awake and watching them curiously.

Jamal followed her gaze and smiled at her daughter. "Cute kid. What's her name?"

"Mia," Carmen answered. "She's two."

Jamal reached into his pocket, pulling out a business card. "Listen, if you ever need a tour guide or just a friendly face, give me a call. I'm an accountant by trade, but I moonlight as a Newnan expert."

Carmen took the card, her fingers brushing against his. She felt a small jolt and quickly pulled back.

"Thank you, Ja-mal," she said, stumbling slightly over his name. "That's very kind of you."

As she climbed back into her car, Carmen called out, "Wave bye to the nice man, Mia."

Mia's small hand waved enthusiastically. "Bye-bye man."

As she drove away, she couldn't help but glance in her rearview mirror, watching Jamal's silhouette grow smaller. "New town, new possibilities," she thought. But was she ready?

Chapter 4
Totally Broke

Carmen Diaz

Carmen sank into her chair at the quaint cafe, grateful for a break from her parental duties. Across from her, her best friend Felicia twirled one of her long goddess braids around her finger as she perused the menu. Lola arrived moments later in a darling mock-neck with her long, dark curls swooped into a high ponytail.

"Finally," Felicia said with a grin.

The server approached just as they drifted into casual conversation.

"I'll have the avocado toast with a poached egg, please," Felicia said, as a big brunch crowd entered the café. From a table across the room, an awkward looking older man in his late-thirties sat frozen mid-sip of his coffee, his gaze openly tracking her every movement. He wore a fitted button-down with the sleeves rolled up, forearms resting casually on the table as if he had nowhere else to be. Intoxicated by how the bold yellow of Felicia's sweater-dress set off her mocha skin tone beautifully, his eyes glued to her.

"Looks like you have an admirer," Lola teased.

“Yeah… he’s not really my type. So let’s not look his way to give him hope.”

They laughed, including the server, and Felicia raised her menu, peeking over the edge like a child playing hide-and-seek, hoping he’d finally get the hint.

Carmen examined her options, torn between indulgence and practicality. "The Belgian waffles sound amazing, but I should probably stick with something healthier."

"Girl, treat yourself," Lola chimed in. "You deserve it after the week you've had."

With a small smile, Carmen relented. "Alright, Belgian waffles it is."

As the server jotted down their orders, Lola's countenance dimmed. "Speaking of rough weeks, you won't believe what Jessica did at work yesterday."

Felicia's interest was kindled. "Spill the tea, honey."

"This woman, I swear," Lola began, her voice low and intense. "She's always running her mouth about everyone in the office. Yesterday, she had the nerve to spread a rumor that I'm gunning for our supervisor's job."

Carmen's brow raised. "That's awful, Lola. Have you talked to HR about it?"

"Not yet. I'm gathering evidence first. But it's not just me she targets. Last week, she told everyone that Mark in accounting is having an affair with his assistant."

"Sounds like a real piece of work," Felicia said, with disdain. "Some people just can't stand to see others succeed."

Carmen nodded, thinking about her own struggles. "It's hard enough dealing with life's challenges without someone actively trying to tear you down."

"Exactly," Lola agreed. "But I'm not going to let her get to me. I've worked too hard to let some gossip-monger ruin my reputation."

Felicia reached her arms across the table, squeezing Lola's hand. "That's the spirit, girl. Kill 'em with success and bury 'em with a smile."

Their food arrived and as Lola and Felicia dug in, Carmen pushed her food around her plate, her appetite waning as she contemplated her own troubles. "Speaking of challenges," she sighed, "I don't know how

I’m going to afford this $200 daycare increase. I'm barely keeping afloat as it is."

Lola's fork clattered against her plate. "Yeah, I remember you mentioning that. That's insane! How are you going to manage that?"

"I don't know," Carmen admitted. "And get this - Tony had the nerve to ask me for money to pay his bills. Meanwhile, he's not helping out with Mia at all."

Felicia's eyes widened in disbelief. "Girl, please tell me you didn't give him a dime."

"No way. But it's tight. I'm..." She hesitated, shame coloring her cheeks.

"What is it, Car?" Lola pressed, leaning in.

"I’m totally broke, no money left over. He has all the dishes. I have one skillet and a rusty pot. And I'm sleeping on an air mattress," Carmen confessed quietly.

"Yeah, I can't believe you're sleeping on an air mattress girl, while his lazy ass is resting peacefully in a bed every night," she frowned.

"What? No, tell me it's not so," Felicia replied, her voice rising with indignation.

“No, she’s not lying. I told her to ask her folks for a loan, but she’s too proud,” Lola replied.

Carmen's eyes stung with unshed tears. "It's not ideal, but I'm making it work. Mia's comfort comes first."

Anger blazed in Felicia's eyes. "Okay, that's it. You need to put Tony on child support, like yesterday."

"I don't know..." Carmen hesitated, her mind racing with potential complications.

"Listen," Felicia insisted, "it'll go through the courts. You won't have to beg him anymore because it'll come straight out of his check."

Lola snorted, rolling her eyes. "What check?"

Carmen couldn't help but chuckle at that, some of the tension easing from her shoulders. "You've got a point there. He can barely hold down a job."

As she considered Felicia's suggestion, Carmen felt a little better. Maybe this could be the solution she needed to provide stability for Mia and herself in their new life in Newnan.

Carmen's phone buzzed against the tabletop, but she ignored it.

Their server appeared again heading to the table behind them.

Felicia's eyes widened appreciatively. "Look at that nice tush on him," she whispered, her gaze following as he walked away.

Carmen rolled her eyes, but couldn't suppress a small smile. "Fe, behave yourself."

Her phone vibrated again, insistent. Lola glanced down, her eyebrows shooting up. "Ooh, Carmen. Jamal's calling."

"I'll just call him back later," Carmen responded quickly.

"Wow! he's thinking about you early in the morning," Lola laughed, checking the time on her phone.

Heat rushed to Carmen's cheeks. "We've been chatting on and off for the past week or so. Sometimes during the day, sometimes in the evening. It's nothing, really."

"Nothing?" Felicia teased, reaching for the phone. "Then you won't mind if I answer?"

Carmen snatched it away. "Don't you dare."

Lola grinned, nudging Carmen's shoulder. "Go on, prima. Answer it. We won't eavesdrop... much."

Torn between embarrassment and a flutter of excitement, Carmen took a deep breath and swiped to answer. "Hey, Jamal," she said, trying to control her tone as her friends exchanged looks across the table.

Carmen turned slightly in her chair, seeking a semblance of privacy. "I'm at a cafe with friends in Rex," she said. "How are you?"

"I'm good. Just wanted to check in. Last time we talked you said you were still unpacking. How are you settling in?"

A smile tugged at Carmen's lips. "It's been... an adjustment. But we're managing."

"Listen," Jamal continued, "I was thinking... if you'd still like, I could show you around Newnan sometime. Help you get more familiar with the place."

"That's really sweet of you, Jamal."

"It'd be my pleasure."

She glanced at Felicia and Lola, who were straining to hear. "Thank you. I'm looking forward to it!"

They talked a few more minutes before ending the call. Felicia pounced immediately. "Okay, spill. What's the tea on this Jamal guy?"

Carmen sighed, setting her phone down. "He's just a friend. Remember when Mia and I were stranded? He's the one who helped us out."

Lola raised an eyebrow. "Just a friend, huh? That's how it always starts."

"Come on," Carmen protested. "It's not like that."

"Well, what's he look like? Give us details, girl," Felicia pressed.

Carmen hesitated, then relented. "He's... handsome. Tall, fine. Has this sexy well-groomed beard and the most expressive eyes." She took note of her friends' faces before continuing. They seemed to have loved everything she'd just said so she resumed. "Six years older. He's thirty-three years old." They raised brows with an impressed grin.

She paused, then added quietly, "He's Black."

Felicia's expression read surprise and concern. "Oh, Carmen," she said softly, "You know how your parents feel about that."

Carmen did know, all too well.

Lola's eyes widened. "Tío will have a fit."

Carmen really liked the vibes she was getting from Jamal, but the thought of another drama-filled relationship wasn't what she needed, ever.

"What does he do for a living? He isn't a social media gamer, like Tony, right?" Lola laughed.

"Or a struggling rapper?" Felicia chimed in, her mouth full of eggs.

Carmen cut off their teasing with a firm tone. "He's an accountant."

Silence fell over the table. Felicia's fork clattered against her plate as she set it down. "Wow," she breathed. "I say keep him and don't tell your dad."

Lola sat back, speechless.

"Look, he and I are just friends."

"Yeah, but how long do you see that lasting?" Lola challenged. "Chicks and guys can't be just friends, Car. You aren't that naive, prima."

Carmen grabbed her fork, loading her mouth with a bite of Belgian waffle to avoid responding. As she chewed, she thought about Jamal's sexy body and gorgeous eyes. 'Just friends,' she told herself firmly. 'It has to be just friends.'

Swallowing, she met her friends' gazes. "Let's just change the subject," she suggested, her voice filled with emotion she couldn't quite hide.

Chapter 5

Never Considered

Jamal Adams

Jamal shivered on the porch, pulling his jacket tighter as a gust of wind blew across his chilled dark skin. The door creaked open, revealing Keyana wearing a cozy oversized sweater paired with leggings and ankle boots.

"Hey big bro, get in here before you freeze," Keyana said, ushering him inside.

Jamal stepped in, whiffing the scent of cinnamon and apples coming from the kitchen. He turned to his sister, taking in her vibrant energy despite the early hour.

"Thanks for letting me in, Key. You're looking good for a Sunday morning."

Keyana rolled her eyes playfully. "Some of us don't roll out of bed looking like a hot mess."

Jamal chuckled, then he became sentimental. "Listen, I really appreciate you staying home this semester to help out with Mom. I know it can't be easy giving up campus life."

"She's my mom too, Jamal. You don't have to thank me for doing what's right."

Jamal was proud of his sister's maturity but he felt a bit of guilt as well. He felt that he should be the one here, taking care of their mother. But Keyana had stepped up without hesitation, putting their mom's needs before her own comfort.

"Still, it means a lot. How's she doing today?"

"Better. She was up early, determined to guide me in making apple pie. I swear, that woman is unstoppable."

The strong scent of apples and cinnamon suddenly made sense. Jamal smiled, picturing his mother rolling around in her wheelchair giving instruction. Some things never changed.

Jamal made his way down the hall to the in-law suite where his mother was recovering from her knee surgery. He paused at the doorway of the room. His mother, Patrice, sat propped up in bed, her hair in two flat twist halo. His father, Millard, occupied the worn armchair beside her with a newspaper in his hand.

"There's Jamal," Patrice smiled.

Jamal entered, giving his mother a gentle hug. "How you feeling, Ma?"

"I miss my bed upstairs. The walls feel like they're closing in, room's too small," she frowned.

"Well, it's only temporary. You'll be able to go back upstairs to your room soon enough," Jamal smiled. "How are you feeling though?"

"Oh, I'm fine," she waved off his concern, but her smile faltered. "It's just... my boss, Jamal. I'm worried they might let me go over this medical leave."

Millard lowered his paper, frowning. "It ain't right, the way they treat folks these days."

Jamal hated seeing his parents stressed. "Don't you worry about that, Ma. They can't fire you for taking necessary medical leave. I'll look into it if there's any trouble."

His father nodded approvingly, then abruptly changed the subject. "Did you see Keyana's grades this semester? That girl's going places."

"Speaking of going places," Patrice chimed in. "how's work treating you, baby? Any interesting clients?"

"Work's good. Got a few new small businesses I'm helping out. And Tavaris is killing it! He might even make partner soon."

He noticed Keyana leaning against the doorframe. "That's great and all," she drawled, "but what we really want to know is... you got a girlfriend yet?"

His family had grown concerned that Jamal hadn't been in anything serious since his breakup with Kelis. His mom would often offer to set him up with young ladies who attended her church, but it had become obvious that he and his mother didn't share the same taste when it came to attractiveness. The women he'd wish his mom would send him on a blind date with she never would, instead she'd fix him up with the ones you'd have to be blind to bear looking at.

Jamal felt heat creep up his neck. "Well, no but there's this sweet Latina..." He found himself smiling as he recounted meeting Carmen. "She was stranded on the side of the road, needed a jump. She's... something else. Beautiful, smart, has this adorable little girl — "

"A child?" His father's brows raised. "Was she married?"

"I... don't think so," Jamal replied, caught off guard by the question.

Millard shook his head. "You know, sometimes other cultures don't care for Black men dating their women."

"Dad," Jamal started, but Keyana cut in.

"Please," she scoffed. "It's plenty of Black and Brown folks my age mixing. Y'all are just old school."

"Girl," Patrice said. "at least you're as smart with your studies as you are with that mouth of yours."

Jamal chuckled, grateful for his sister's intervention, even as he did feel a twinge of worry about the situation. He hadn't considered how his parents might react to Carmen's background.

Jamal's phone buzzed, Carmen's name lighting up the screen.

"Hey, Carmen," he answered, stepping out onto the porch. The crisp winter air nipped at his cheeks.

"Hi Jamal," Carmen's voice was warm, but hesitant. "We're still on for today, right?"

"Absolutely. I'm looking forward to it." He glanced at his watch. "I'll head out now."

Jamal stepped back into the house and told his parents and Keyana goodbye before leaving to meet up with Carmen. As Jamal slid into his car, he thought about his parents' concerns about him getting involved with Carmen. He shook them off, focusing on the road ahead.

•••••••••••

The Starbucks in Newnan was busy when he arrived. Carmen waved from a corner table, her curly blonde hair catching the afternoon sun. Jamal's breath caught in his throat.

"I hope you don't mind, I ordered us some pumpkin spice lattes," Carmen said as he sat down.

"Perfect for the weather," Jamal smiled, noting the nervousness in her eyes. "How's your day been?"

They chatted easily, continuing the conversations they'd already started over the phone during the past few weeks. Carmen's eyes lit up when she spoke about her daughter.

"Mia's the light of my life," she smiled. "She's so curious about everything."

Jamal hesitated, then asked, "Were you married to Mia's father?"

Carmen's smile faltered. "No, we... we recently broke up. I moved here from Rex, where Tony and I shared an apartment."

"Why'd you break up?" The words tumbled out before Jamal could stop them.

"It just wasn't working," Carmen replied, her eyes dropping to her latte.

Jamal wondered if he was overstepping, but he needed to know. "What about Mia? Does she miss Tony? You said his name is Tony, right?"

Carmen shifted uncomfortably. "I'm sure he'll see her soon," she said, her tone clipped.

Jamal sensed he'd hit a nerve. He wanted to apologize, to change the subject, but Carmen's discomfort gnawed at him. What wasn't she telling him?

Jamal cleared his throat, eager to shift the conversation. "So, what do you like to do for fun around here?"

Carmen's shoulders relaxed visibly. "I love exploring the parks with Mia. There's this beautiful spot in Greenville Street Park with a fountain. It's so peaceful."

"I know that place," Jamal nodded. "The dogwoods there are gorgeous in spring."

As they talked, Jamal found himself drawn to Carmen's bold hair and her gorgeous face. Her eyes looked beautiful when she laughed, but he had to remind himself to focus on friendship.

"What about you?" Carmen asked. "Any hidden talents?"

Jamal chuckled. "Well, I'm pretty good at grilling. My friends always volunteer me for cookouts."

"Oh, I'd love to try your cooking sometime," Carmen blushed slightly.

"Maybe we can arrange that. As friends, of course."

They finished their coffees, chatting about their favorite spots in Newnan. As they stood to leave, Jamal gestured toward his car. "Ready for that tour of Newnan I've been meaning to give you?"

Carmen hesitated, eyeing his Infinity. "It's a nice car," she said, her voice tight.

"Thanks," Jamal replied, noticing her unease. "We can walk if you prefer."

"No, it's okay," Carmen said, taking a deep breath. "Let's go."

As they got in, Jamal turned on some smooth R&B. Carmen visibly relaxed, tapping her fingers to the beat.

"The Coweta County African American Heritage Museum is just down the road," Jamal suggested. "Have you been?"

Carmen shook her head, a smile spreading across her face. "That sounds perfect."

•••••••••••

Carmen's eyes lit up as she absorbed the rich history surrounding her at the museum. As they stood in front of the African American art piece, Jamal couldn't help but steal glances at her. The way the light played off her golden beige skin was captivating, highlighting every gorgeous feature of her face. Her brown eyes sparkled as she engaged with the artwork, inviting him to get lost in her thoughts.

He noticed everything about her-the way her sweater hugged her curves, the fabric accentuating her body in the most flattering way. The jeans she wore complemented her ass perfectly, and he found himself momentarily mesmerized by how effortlessly she carried herself, radiating virtue and grace. Her giggles were infectious, pulling a smile from his lips that he didn't even realize was there.

"I'm really enjoying today."

"So am I, friend."

They continued through the museum, pausing to examine photographs and read plaques. Carmen found herself laughing at Jamal's witty observations, her usual caution melting away in his presence. As they moved from one piece to another, their conversation flowed effortlessly. He admired how deeply she appreciated the art, her insights bringing a fresh perspective that made him respect her even more. She had a way of making every topic feel lively and fascinating, and he loved the enthusiasm in her voice as she expressed her thoughts. It was rare to find someone who not only was beautiful but also had a passion for conversation that ignited the room around them. He hadn't felt like this about anyone in years. Not since... Kelis. A woman like Carmen was undoubtedly rare these days. Ms. Diaz was definitely someone Jamal wanted to see more of.

"So, where would you like me to take you next time we hang out?"

"Oh, you want to see me again?"

"Certainly," Jamal replied. "Isn't that what friends do?"

"Why don't you pick the place?" she suggested, pushing aside her conflicted feelings. "You did so well this time."

"I'd be honored. I'll make sure it's something special."

As they moved on to the next exhibit, Carmen found herself wondering what Jamal had in mind. She couldn't remember the last time she'd felt this excited about spending time with someone who wasn't Mia.

For Jamal, everything about that day with Carmen was a whole vibe- the intimate atmosphere of the museum, the shared experience of discovering art, and the connection sparking between them. The shared smiles and lingering glances said it all. Something special was definitely going on. As he listened to her excited descriptions, he couldn't help but feel lucky to be on this date, getting to know not just the art but also her personality, and seeing a clearer picture of who she really was.

••••●•●•••

Jamal sank into his couch, the events of the day replaying in his mind. He couldn't shake the image of Carmen's smile, the way her eyes lit up as they explored the museum together. With a deep breath, he pulled out his phone and dialed Tavaris.

"Yo, what's good?" Tavaris's smooth voice came through the speaker.

"Man, you won't believe the day I had," Jamal said, unable to keep the excitement from his voice. "Remember that woman I helped with her car? Carmen? We hung out today."

Tavaris let out a low whistle. "For real? How'd it go?"

Jamal leaned back, grinning. "It was... amazing. She's gorgeous, T. Smart, funny, the whole package."

"Hold up," Tavaris interjected. "Is she hotter than Brandi?"

"Hotter," Jamal replied without hesitation.

"Booty and all? What about the face card?"

Jamal rolled his eyes, but his smile didn't fade. "Face card is exceptional, man."

"You didn't say the booty was shaking right," Tavaris pressed.

Jamal sighed, his tone growing serious. "Hey, she's a winner. That's good enough for you to know."

There was a pause on the other end of the line. Jamal could almost hear Tavaris's gears turning.

"So... since you're going for Carmen," Tavaris began, cautiously, "you mind if I take a shot with Brandi?"

Jamal chuckled, shaking his head. "She's all yours, man."

As he hung up, Jamal's thoughts drifted back to Carmen. He knew he should take things slow, focus on friendship. But he couldn't deny the connection he felt. With a sigh, he closed his eyes, allowing himself to imagine what could be.

Chapter 6

Quid pro quo

Carmen Diaz

The wind nipped at Carmen's hands as she unbuckled Mia from her car seat. A faint smile touched her face recalling her museum visit with Jamal a few days ago, but it disappeared as she snapped back to reality. She hugged her daughter close, shielding her from the cold, as she hurried up the short pathway to their tiny rental house. Once inside, she set Mia down on the small brown faux-leather loveseat against the wall. Mia's eyes lit up at the sight of the TV in the corner.

"TV, Mama!" Mia exclaimed, pointing excitedly towards the small screen.

As Mia watched television, Carmen thought about what she had to barter in order for Tony to bring Mia's old television over last week. "*I'll bring it over... what are you gonna give me when I get there?*"

The memory of what he said kept popping up in her head. She had felt trapped then, just like every time she needed him for help. He only ever stepped up to help when there was something in it for him, something that left her feeling used or dirty.

Carmen clenched her fists. It wasn't just about the TV; it was about their daughter. Every time Tony dangled money or support, it came with strings . The idea of sleeping with him, even for the sake of her daughter, gnawed at her conscience. It felt like a trade-off, like her body was the currency for his duplicitous generosity.

She shook her head, trying to dispel the memory. "Yeah, baby. We can watch a little TV while Mama makes dinner."

As Carmen moved to the kitchenette, her eyes fell on the stack of bills on the counter. The daycare invoice glared . Carmen stood there trying to figure out how she would pull off paying the bills every month on her own. Though Tony had been only marginally helpful in managing their household expenses, the safety net of having someone else around, even a lackluster partner, was now gone. The utilities, groceries, and rent were solely on her now. As she stared into her near-empty fridge, she knew even the food she bought today would have to be stretched. Carmen was overwhelmed by the harsh reality of single parenthood. The decisions she had made, in hopes of a better life for herself and her child, now seemed fraught with uncertainty. Her paycheck stretched barely far enough to cover the essentials. She worried about how to manage not just the financial burden, but the emotional weight of ensuring that Mia felt safe and secure now that her family structure had changed. Carmen couldn't help but ponder whether her leaving Tony was a step towards freedom or simply a precursor to hardship.

"Fifty extra dollars a week. How am I supposed to afford that?"

She glanced back at Mia, babbling at the cartoon characters on the screen.

"I can't believe he won't take care of his own daughter unless I ..." She brushed the thought from her mind, unable to finish it aloud.

Carmen started thinking about Jamal instead, and how different he was from Tony. What would he think if he knew she was still sleeping with Tony?

"I gotta end this," she whispered to herself. "For Mia. For me."

As she looked around at the loveseat Lola had bought out of pity and the TV that came at such a steep price, it all just reinforced her feelings of failure.

"Mia, baby, Mama's gotta get the groceries. You stay put, okay?"

"'Kay," Mia replied, eyes glued to the colorful characters dancing across the screen.

Carmen stepped outside. The wind bit at her cheeks as she popped the trunk, to get the bags of groceries. As Carmen shuttled between the car and the house, Mia's little face peered over the back of the loveseat each time the door swung open.

"Cold, Mama!" Mia exclaimed, shivering despite her zipped-up coat.

"I'm sorry, baby. Mama's almost done."

Finally, she brought in the last bag, kicking the door shut behind her.

"Can't believe I spent this damn much and still don't have a full week of groceries," she grumbled, eyeing the crumpled receipt.

"Potty, Mama," Mia announced, squirming on the loveseat.

"Coming, sweetie."

Carmen pulled Mia's coat off, then took her to the potty. After putting Mia into the playpen, Carmen cranked up the thermostat. "I gotta figure out how to save on energy, but she already seems like she's trying to catch a cold."

Carmen grabbed a tissue, gently wiping her daughter's snotty nose. "What am I gonna do, baby girl?" she whispered, more to herself than to Mia. "How are we gonna make it?"

Carmen headed back into the kitchen to prepare dinner. She stood at the counter, chopping cilantro and onions for the quesadillas she was making. As she pulled out the tortillas, she thought of taking on extra hours at work to help pay the bills. But the reality that she would end up needing to hire a babysitter for those hours reminded her that anything she did to earn extra money while she was living on her own with Mia, would be a catch-22. Feeling defeated, Carmen turned back to the stove, heating the skillet while trying to come up with other options. Just as she melted cheese onto the tortillas, Mia burst into giggles, momentarily easing the stress in Carmen's head.

The phone rung. Carmen glanced at the caller ID. It was Jamal.

"Hey there," she answered.

"Carmen, how's it going?"

She cradled the phone between her ear and shoulder, reaching for the sauté pan for the vegetables. "Oh, I'm good. Making dinner for the munchkin."

"Listen," Jamal continued, "I was thinking... maybe we could catch a movie this weekend?"

"Sounds fun, but I'll have to let you know later. Depends on whether I can get a babysitter."

"Oh, right." A pause. "No worries, just thought I'd ask."

She could hear the disappointment in his voice. "I'm sorry, Jamal. It's just..."

"Hey, I get it," he assured her. "You've got responsibilities."

As they chatted, Carmen stirred the vegetables absently, thinking about how Jamal was so understanding, so patient. But she remembered him telling her that he'd never dated a mom before. The women he dated were likely always available at a whelm. She couldn't help but worry that her not being able to be as spontaneous as the women he was accustomed to, would eventually pose a problem if they ever became more than friends.

They said their goodbyes, and Carmen hung up, feeling a bit insecure. She'd barely set the phone down when it rang again. Tony's name flashed on the screen. He was definitely the last person she wanted to talk to right now, but he was Mia's dad.

"Yeah, what's going on Tony?"

"Hey Car. You still need a little money for daycare?"

Carmen's breath caught. "Of course! You got it?"

"Yeah, gotcha babe. You got me?" His voice dropped, sounding really thirsty.

"Tony, are you asking me to fuck you for daycare money?"

"Hey, we both got needs while we're single and co-parenting, right?"

Carmen closed her eyes, conflicting emotions warring within her. "When are you bringing the money?"

"Be there in about two hours. Put on something sexy for me."

As the line went dead, Carmen stared at the phone, feeling dirty and desperate. How had it come to this? She felt as if she were prostituting to pay her bills. She didn't want to be with Tony anymore. She loved him, but she no longer respected him and she sure as hell didn't feel as if he respected her. Having sex with him was the last thing she wanted to do. But, it seemed as if that was all she could do to make it. There wasn't any other alternative that she could think of.

Carmen got Mia fed and bathed so that she could get her daughter to sleep and be ready when Tony got there.

Carmen's fingers trembled as she buttoned up Mia's pajamas. "There you go, baby girl. "Time for bed."

Mia yawned, her eyelids heavy. "Story, Mama?"

"Not tonight, sweetie. Mama's got... something to do."

After tucking Mia in, Carmen searched through the storage container that she was using as a temporary dresser. She pulled out a pair of pink thongs and a colorful sweatshirt. Carmen changed quickly, the doorbell rang shortly after. She opened the door.

"Hey, sexy," Tony grinned, licking his lips as his eyes roamed her body.

"Where's the money?" Carmen blurted out.

Tony's smile faltered. "Damn, Car. You tryin' to play me?"

"Play you?" Carmen's voice rose. "You think sex is more important than our daughter's daycare?"

"Whoa, chill." Tony raised his hands. "I've got the money. Just thought we could, y'know, have fun first. We hardly see each other anymore, Car. I miss you."

His hands found her waist. "You're so damn sexy."

As Tony's lips met hers, warmth spread through Carmen's body. Part of her wanted to believe his lies just one more time. His hand slid under her sweatshirt. She kissed him back as they stumbled towards the small brown loveseat. Clothes were hastily discarded, their bodies intertwining on the cold fabric. It didn't take long for the cold surface to warm up from their body heat.

As she laid back and Tony adjusted his body between her thighs, Carmen closed her eyes. Instead of Tony's scent, she imagined Jamal's cologne. Her hands explored Tony's body, but in her mind, it was Jamal's smooth dark skin beneath her fingertips. As he stroked her, she wished that it was Jamal inside her.

"Damn, Car," Tony grunted. "It's never been this good."

Carmen bit her lip, guilt and pleasure warring within her. "Shh," she whispered. "Mia's asleep."

Their encounter was intense and over quickly. As they lay tangled on the loveseat, Carmen felt sick. The sex had been satisfying, but everything else felt wrong. It was over between her and Tony. She didn't want to be doing this. He didn't appreciate her, nor did he deserve her-not her love, or her body.

Tony reached for his pants, pulling out a wad of cash. "Here," he said, handing her $250. "For daycare."

Carmen's eyes widened. "How can you afford this?"

Tony shrugged. "Went full-time at work. Had to, to cover rent without you."

"Oh." Carmen clutched the money, conflicted.

"Listen, Car," Tony leaned in. "You need to bring your ass back home. Stop playin'. Mia deserves a whole family."

Carmen sighed. "Tony— "

"We can make this shit work," he insisted. "I'm tryin', babe."

Carmen heard what Tony was saying. It sounded good, but she'd heard it too many times before. She was tired of hearing that shit now.

"No. We can't."

"Car—"

"It's time for me to be on my own, Tony. Mia will have us both, just... not together."

Chapter 7

Mounting Expenses

Carmen Diaz

Carmen stood in front of the mirror on the back of her bedroom door, combing her long blonde hair as she got ready for her shift at the pharmacy. The $250 Tony had given her eight days ago barely made a dent in her mounting expenses. Utilities, groceries, car payments, insurance - it all seemed to pile up. It was just too expensive for one damn person. And now, with Mia's recent bout of flu, things had only gotten worse.

The co-payments at the doctor's office and prescription fees had taken a significant chunk out of her already meager bank balance. Missing two days of work to care for Mia had been the final blow. Now, she was short for March's rent.

Her eyes shifted from her reflection to Mia, who sat at the end of Carmen's bed, a piece that Carmen bought a week ago from a used furniture store. Mia was coughing and sniffling. Her usually bright eyes were glassy with fever and her cheeks were flushed.

"Your medicine should bring down your fever in a few minutes, okay sweetie."

Mia nodded pouty faced, clutching her stuffed rabbit. "Kay."

She glanced at her phone, silently thanking God for Felicia. Her best friend had agreed to babysit Mia while working from home, a small mercy in this storm of financial stress.

"Come on, mija," Carmen said, forcing a smile. "Let's get you to Tía Felicia's."

As they made their way to the car, Carmen tried to figure out potential solutions. She could ask for extra shifts at the pharmacy, but that would mean less time with Mia and possibly having to pay a babysitter if she had to work outside of daycare hours. Maybe she could sell some of her jewelry? But the thought of parting with the few precious items she owned made her heart ache.

The stress of it all pressed down on her shoulders as she buckled Mia into her car seat. She'd thought she could manage on her own, away from Tony's unreliability. But now, faced with the harsh reality of her situation, doubt crept in.

Carmen drove to Felicia's house, her mind spinning with thoughts about going back to Tony. As much as she hated to admit it, the money he had given her was more than she could scrape together on her own right now. It was almost if Tony's not good enough while they were together had actually been worth something after all. Maybe she could swallow her pride and move back in with him, at least until she got back on her feet financially. They were still sleeping together anyway.

But even as the idea crossed her mind, she knew it was a fool's errand. It wasn't just the money she needed to think about. She had been miserable with Tony. He was lazy, manipulative, inconsiderate, and disrespectful. Tony would never change. She had seen that time and again over the years. A few hundred bucks here and there didn't make up for his chronic unreliability and selfishness. And she refused to put Mia through the instability of living with someone like him again.

No, going back wasn't really an option. She would just have to figure this out, like she always did. Carmen was shaken from her thoughts as she pulled up to Felicia's cute little 3 bedroom ranch. She unbuckled

Mia from the car seat and carried the sniffling toddler to the front door.

Felicia welcomed them in cheerfully. "Hey girl! And hi Miss Mia!" she said, giving Carmen a quick hug before taking Mia into her arms. "Auntie Felicia has got lots of fun stuff planned for you today!"

Carmen smiled gratefully at her friend as Felicia showed her the fold-away- bed and TV she had set up for Mia in the office. On top of it all, Felicia had even gotten Mia a gift bag with new dolls and toy food to play with. Carmen really appreciated how thoughtful and supportive her best friend was.

"Thank you so much Fe," she said, giving Felicia another tight hug. "You're a lifesaver."

She kissed Mia's head and told her to be good, then went over the medicine schedule and instructions with Felicia. After one more round of thank yous, Carmen headed out the door to start her pharmacy shift, determined to power through and figure out a solution.

•••••••••••

Carmen arrived at the pharmacy, her mind still preoccupied with all her troubles. As she clocked in and donned her white lab coat, she struggled to focus on the tasks at hand.

The first customer's prescription should have been a routine task, but Carmen found herself distracted, nearly mislabeling the medication bottle. She caught the mistake just in time, but the close call left her flustered.

Later, while counting out pills for another customer's order, she spilled several capsules onto the countertop. Carmen quickly scooped them back into the bottle, but the customer had already witnessed the mishap.

"What's going on here?" the man demanded, his voice laced with frustration. "I don't want those pills after they've been on the counter!"

Carmen apologized profusely, her cheeks flushing with embarrassment as she retrieved a new bottle and carefully counted out the correct dosage.

The pharmacist, Mr. Hancock, had been observing the commotion from his office. He emerged, his brow furrowed with concern. "Carmen, can I see you for a moment?"

She followed him into the small office, afraid that her job was going to be on the line if she made another mistake.

"What's going on with you today?" Mr. Hancock asked. "You've already been out two days this week, and now you're making careless mistakes with customer orders. That's not like you."

Carmen's eyes dropped to the floor, ashamed. She knew she had screwed up badly, and the repercussions could be severe if she continued making such glaring errors.

"I'm sorry, Mr. Hancock. I've had a lot on my mind lately, with Mia being sick and... financial troubles. But that's no excuse. I'll do better, I promise."

"I understand things have been tough for you, Carmen. But you know I can't have these kinds of mistakes happening on the floor. People's health and safety are at stake."

He paused, letting his words sink in. "I'll let it slide for today, but you need to get your head back in the game. I'll be watching closely, and if I see any more careless errors, we'll have to re-evaluate your position here."

"Thank you, Mr. Hancock. It won't happen again."

As she exited the office and returned to her workstation, Carmen took a deep breath, forcing herself to clear her mind of the distractions that had plagued her all morning. She knew Mr. Hancock would be keeping a close eye on her performance for the rest of the day, and she couldn't afford any more slip-ups.

When Carmen clocked out for lunch, she grabbed her purse out of the locker and checked her phone. A smile crossed her face as she saw Felicia's message about Mia's improved condition. She said that Mia was having the time of her life playing with the dolls and play food she'd given her that morning. The image of her daughter giggling and playing made Carmen feel a lot better about how the day was going.

Her relief was short-lived, however, as she noticed Tony's text. The offer of $75 towards utilities in exchange for some pussy. "*Maybe put on that pink bodysuit you know I like,*" his text continued. She knew what it meant, what he expected, and the idea made her nauseous.

As she scrolled further, Jamal's message caught her eye, "*Morning beautiful. Hope you and Mia have a great day today and that she feels better. Let me know if you need anything, especially with missing work those days.*" His words were so opposite of Tony's. He was genuine, caring, and without any apparent ulterior motives. Carmen wondered if his offer of help extended to financial support. The thought both intrigued and unsettled her, as she wasn't used to kindness without strings attached.

Walking to her car, Carmen dialed Felicia's number. As she listened to her friend's positive report about Mia, she started to feel a lot calmer. Hearing Mia's voice, still a bit raspy but undeniably cheerful, made her smile.

After ending the call, Carmen sat in her car, staring at Tony's message. Reluctantly she typed out a reply:

"*See you Thursday Tony.*" She felt disgusted as she hit send, knowing what she was agreeing to.

Carmen started the engine to drive to Burger King. She was relieved about Mia's recovery, disgusted at Tony's proposition, and curious about Jamal's offer. This thing with Tony was like being trapped in a cycle she couldn't seem to escape.

Carmen pulled up to the drive-thru at Burger King and placed her order, a whopper combo with a coke and a chocolate sundae. She needed the sugar with all the stress she was under. As she pulled up to the pay window, her phone rang. It was Jamal.

"Hey," she answered. "Hold on a sec." She paid, and then resumed the call.

"I was just calling because I hadn't heard from you. I'd texted earlier seeing if you were alright or needed anything," he mentioned.

She grabbed her meal and headed to a parking space. "Yeah, I saw...just been so busy at work, hectic. Covid and flu season..."

"So, how's Mia?"

"She's better. My friend Felicia is watching her today since she's working from home."

They talked for a while with Jamal beating around the bush until he finally asked her how she was doing financially this week after doctor's bills and missing work. Carmen tried to downplay it for a while, but eventually came clean, telling him her situation.

"You're short on rent? Wow! Look, I can loan you money."

Carmen knew if he loaned her money it would be a relief now but paying him back would be a burden later, and more nights with Tony. "I-"

"Look, don't worry about paying me back. Would $350 help?" he offered.

Carmen was caught off guard by the unexpected offer. Part of her wanted to jump at the chance to solve her immediate financial crisis, but another part felt guilty about accepting such generosity. She glanced at the greasy Burger King bag on the passenger seat, suddenly feeling foolish for indulging in fast food when she couldn't even make rent.

Jamal waited patiently on the other end of the line, giving Carmen space to process his offer. He understood her hesitation, having seen firsthand how proud and independent she was. But he also knew she was in a tight spot and genuinely wanted to help.

As Carmen wrestled with her decision, she thought about Mia and the stability she desperately wanted to provide for her daughter. She thought about Tony and the compromises she'd been making just to keep their heads above water. Then she thought about kind, dependable Jamal and how he'd offered her help with no strings attached.

Carmen felt anxious as she considered Jamal's offer. She wanted to prove her independence, but her current financial struggles made it increasingly difficult to turn down his generous help.

"Thank you, Jamal," she said, her voice trembling slightly. "I want to say no, but I can't. I need the help. Are you sure there are no strings attached?"

Jamal chuckled. "Of course there are. Nothing's free."

Carmen felt highly disappointed as she braced herself for the inevitable catch. How could she have been so dumb and naive to think that he would be any different from Tony? She had hoped, if only for a moment, that Jamal's kindness was truly unconditional. Did he want her to screw him too? "What's the string?"

"Just keep being you, and a great mom to Mia," Jamal said, "and don't be afraid to ask for help in the future. That's what friends are for, right?"

Carmen was taken aback by his response. She had expected some hidden agenda, some request for a favor in return. But Jamal's words were genuine, his concern for her and Mia's wellbeing guileless.

"Jamal, I..." Carmen paused, struggling to find the right words. 'How is it that Mr. Right showed up when everything in my life is all wrong?' She shook her head in disbelief. 'What could I possibly have to offer this man?' "There must be something I could offer you for your generosity?"

"You don't have to offer me anything, Carmen. I'm not looking for anything in return, except maybe your continued friendship. You and Mia deserve to have someone in your corner, someone who can be there for you without expectations."

Carmen had been so accustomed to Tony's manipulations and empty promises that the idea of someone genuinely wanting to help, without any ulterior motives, was almost foreign to her.

"Jamal, I..." she began, her voice trembling with emotion. "Thank you. I don't know what to say. This means so much to me, to Mia. I just... I don't want you to get the wrong idea, though. I'm not ready for anything more than friendship right now."

"I understand, Carmen," Jamal replied. "Take all the time you need. I'm just glad I can be here for you and Mia, in whatever way you need. That's what matters to me."

"Okay," she said, a small smile forming on her lips. "I'll accept your help, Jamal. Thank you, from the bottom of my heart."

Chapter 8

Here and Now

Jamal Adams

After leaving the Italian pizzeria, Carmen and Jamal headed to the movies in his Infiniti. A popular R&B song came on the radio—Luther Vandross' "Here and Now." In that moment, Carmen and Jamal both felt something stir up in them that they couldn't deny within themselves, and they could sense that the other was feeling it too, but wasn't ready to reveal it.

Jamal decided to diffuse the intense sexual tension by bringing up a laughable moment from the restaurant. "So, about that string of cheese you had stuck to your chin..." he teased, glancing at her with a playful grin.

Carmen rolled her eyes, but a smile tugged at the corners of her mouth. "Well, it was very cheesy," she defended, unable to hide her amusement.

"What about the fact that you had five slices, huh? Plus mozzarella sticks."

"Yeah, that was kind of greedy of me," Jamal admitted, laughing.

Carmen was so grateful to be with a man who made her laugh instead of one who wrecked her nerves, like Tony. She was still irritated from the dick pic he'd sent earlier that morning. Perhaps it would have been a little more interesting if he were packing a tad bit more equipment. As if Thursday's smashing session wasn't enough. Tony volunteered to keep Mia next weekend if Carmen wanted to pick up an extra shift at the pharmacy. It was a shame that Carmen had to perform sexual favors just for Tony to take care of Mia.

Seems like he'd be volunteering to keep Mia since he didn't see her as much now that she and Mia had moved to Newnan. However, a part of him relished the empty nest, except for having to pay all the bills on his own.

Jamal and Carmen pulled up to the movie theater, the parking lot was packed. Jamal came around to Carmen's door, opening it for her just as he had at the pizzeria. "Button that coat before you get out, it's chillier now than it was twenty minutes ago," he warned.

Carmen followed his advice, securing the buttons on her coat before stepping out. She placed both hoods on her head, one from her coat and the other from her aqua blue jogging set. Jamal couldn't help but admire the way the fitted joggers hugged Carmen's curves, accentuating her shapely backside. He was grateful she didn't go for the extra baggy look.

Jamal took Carmen's hand as they made their way to the ticket booth. "Two for 'The Man With the Glass Eye,'" he requested, opting for the thriller over the romantic comedy playing, as they were 'just friends.'

Their tickets were checked and torn once they entered the lobby. Carmen insisted on buying the popcorn since Jamal had paid for everything else that evening. Jamal hesitated for a moment but ultimately agreed, recognizing how important it was for her to contribute.

Carmen and Jamal made their way to the crowded concession stand. The savory aroma of buttery popcorn smelled irresistible .

"Ooh, I'm getting nachos too. I love nachos," Carmen said, reading the menu boards overhead.

"I don't know where you put it all. I'm still stuffed."

"That's because you ate 5 slices of pizza, plus sides," Carmen giggled.

They inched forward in line. Carmen tapped her unmanicured nails on the countertop, debating whether to get a large or extra-large popcorn.

When they reached the register, the bored-looking teen behind the counter asked , "What can I get for you?"

"Let's do a large popcorn, nachos with extra cheese, and two Cokes," Carmen responded.

As the teen punched in their order, Jamal leaned in and said softly, "Make sure they don't skimp on the butter."

Carmen smiled. "I like the way you think."

They moved down to the end of the counter to wait for their food. Jamal glanced around at the crowd.

"Packed house tonight," he commented. "Must be because of the new movie."

"I know, I haven't seen it this busy in awhile."

Their order was called out, and Jamal grabbed the tray of food. Carmen reached for her wallet to pay.

"You sure you don't want me to get this?"

"I'm sure," Carmen insisted, handing the cashier her card. "You've paid for everything else this evening."

"Alright, but next time it's on me," Jamal conceded with a smile.

"Deal," she agreed happily as they turned to make their way towards their theater.

The dimly lit theater added to the intensity of the movie. "The Man With the Glass Eye" lived up to its thriller billing, keeping both Carmen and Jamal on the edge of their seats. But the real excitement wasn't playing out on the silver screen.

As Carmen reached for another handful of popcorn, her fingers brushed against Jamal's. They both definitely felt the chemistry, but quickly pulled away, pretending not to notice. This dance repeated itself throughout the movie.

During a particularly suspenseful scene, the villain crept closer to the unsuspecting victim. Carmen, caught up in the moment, instinctively grabbed Jamal's arm as if he was her protector. Little did Jamal know, Carmen was beginning to see him as just that. In these moments of fear and vulnerability, she found herself turning to him for safety. Yet, a part of her resisted these growing feelings, afraid to open herself up to potential hurt again.

As the credits rolled, they made their way out of the theater, both slightly dazed from the intensity of the film and the feelings stirring inside them. Jamal drove Carmen back to the pizzeria where her car waited.

"Thanks for a great evening," Carmen said softly as they pulled up.

She leaned in for a hug, and Jamal savored the feeling of her up against him. Her soft body fit perfectly in his arms. At 5'4" and 140 pounds, Carmen was beautifully proportioned - a small waist, average breasts, and a pleasingly 'plump enough' ass that caught Jamal's attention without being overly dramatic.

As they parted, Jamal couldn't help but wonder why Carmen always insisted on meeting him out rather than allowing him to pick her up from home. Even when he'd helped her with the rent money, they'd met at a coffee shop. He'd never seen her place, nor had she visited his. He assumed that maybe she didn't trust him fully yet, or she didn't trust herself to be alone with him. Either way, he respected it and wanted to go at her pace to insure she was comfortable.

Jamal pulled out of the parking lot of the pizzeria feeling content after his evening with Carmen, though his mind was spinning with thoughts of her. He couldn't stop thinking about the chemistry he felt whenever they touched, even just the slightest brush of her hand. There was an undeniable connection between them that he wanted to explore further but he knew he had to take things slow.

•••••••••••

Jamal decided to stop by his parents' house to see how his mom, Patrice, was recovering from her recent knee surgery. His sister Keyana answered the door.

"Hey big bro! I thought I heard you pull up," she said, giving him a quick hug. As they pulled away, Keyana noticed a smudge of lipstick near the collar on his jacket.

"Oh, is that Carmen's lipstick on your jacket? You guys must have gotten pretty cozy tonight," Keyana teased.

"No, nothing like that. We just hugged goodbye and I guess some of her lipstick must have rubbed off."

"Mmhmm...a hug, that's all? How many dates have you and Carmen had so far and still no kissing yet?"

Jamal shook his head, amused by his sister's nosiness. Keyana was always so blunt and new school in her thinking. She didn't understand taking things slowly, building a friendship first before pursuing anything romantic.

Eager to change the subject, Jamal asked, "How's Mom doing? Is she upstairs resting?" Jamal's mom had recently insisted that her husband Millard take her to their room because the in-law suite downstairs made her feel claustrophobic. He was glad she was only 160 pounds, but his back was aching for three days after, none the less.

"She's doing a lot better today. Her and Dad are up in their room if you want to say hi." Jamal nodded yes and they headed upstairs.

Jamal knocked gently before entering his parents' bedroom. His mom, Patrice, was propped up in bed reading while his dad, Millard, sat in a chair beside her.

"Hey Mom, hey Dad," Jamal greeted, going over to give his mom a kiss on the cheek.

"Hi sweetie, so nice of you to stop by."

They made small talk for awhile, discussing his mom's recovery and how his dad was handling things at work. Eventually the conversation turned to Jamal's personal life.

"So I heard you and Keyana talking about your date with Carmen tonight," Patrice smirked. "Got her lipstick on your coat apparently. You sure did have a nice time, didn't you?"

"Yeah we grabbed a bite to eat and saw a movie. It was fun."

Before he could elaborate further, his dad chimed in with a warning. "Now son, you need to be real careful dating a single mother. I dated a single mom once before your mother and let me tell you..."

Millard went on to tell a long, rambling story about an experience from his younger years. "And she was still bumping and grinding with her baby's father," he shuck his head. "Plus, if you marry her, you automatically become financially responsible for that kid till it's 18 years old."

Patrice gave her husband a weary look. "Oh he won't marry her. Our Jamal is smarter than that, Millard."

Jamal just nodded, taking in his father's words of caution. He appreciated his dad looking out for him, but knew in his heart he needed to follow his own path with Carmen, wherever it led.

When he was done visiting with his parents, Keyana walked Jamal back downstairs to the front door. She talked low this time so that their parents couldn't eavesdrop.

"Look big bro, it's obvious that you are really feelin' this Carmen chick," Keyana grinned. "Be careful like Dad said, but also remember that life is short. You gotta live it while you got it to live. If you want to explore this thing with Carmen, go for it. It's your life, not Mom's and Daddy's."

"Thanks Sis," Jamal smiled. "You are wise beyond your years Key."

"I know. See you later bro."

Jamal thought about what his parents warned and then about Keyana telling him to go for it. He really wanted to go for it. But, there was a part of him that now needed to know where things stood with Carmen and her ex, Tony before he continued to get invested in her. There was no way he wanted to end up in a situation like what his dad described where the object of his affection was still smashing her ex.

Chapter 9

The Park Concert

Carmen Diaz

It was a breezy March Saturday. Jamal hung out with Carmen and Mia at Greenville Street Park. There was a concert for kids there. The characters from one of Mia's favorite cartoons were performing songs from the show. Mia was having the time of her life, dancing and singing along without a care in the world.

Carmen couldn't help but stare at the man that was making her and her daughter's life so happy. She hoped Jamal would stay in their lives for a long time, even though she wasn't ready to become more than just friends yet. He was so good with Mia and Mia really liked Jamal as well. Carmen didn't want to admit it, but Jamal was actually better with Mia than Tony was.

Tony. Carmen couldn't stop thinking about the phone conversation she'd had with Jamal where he'd asked her if she had feelings for Tony still and where things stood with them. She hadn't been fully honest. Things stood nowhere between her and Tony, except for the fact that she was still sleeping with him occasionally. Although there was nothing official between her and Jamal, there was no way Carmen wanted him to find out she was still sleeping with her ex.

Carmen smiled as she watched Mia bop excitedly to the upbeat music blaring from the stage. She bounced on her toes, pigtails flying, as she babbled along to every word the squirrels and birds were singing.

"Go Mia! Dance!" Jamal cheered, clapping to the beat.

Mia turned and gave him a big grin. She opened up her arms signaling Jamal to take her and dance. Mia and Jamal jumped up and down. Jamal chuckled and allowed himself to be gestured closer to the stage by Carmen's very determined toddler.

Carmen watched from afar. She loved seeing Mia so carefree and happy. She had been through so much disruption recently, but days like this helped make up for it.

"Mal dancing!" Mia shouted excitedly over the music to grab Carmen's attention as Jamal broke out some silly moves.

"I see that, baby!" Carmen called back, holding her laughter. "Y'all are doing great!"

The song changed to one from the TV show that Mia clearly knew by heart. She had Jamal to put her down so that she could really show off her dance skills. She belted out every word, jumping and twirling with endless energy. Jamal gamely kept up, laughing as he tried to copy the toddler's dance moves.

When the song ended, Mia ran through the grass back to the chair that Carmen was seated on, giggling uncontrollably. Jamal pretended to wipe sweat from his brow.

"Whew, that wore me out!" he joked. "You've got some moves, short stuff!"

Mia giggled and did a little curtsey before jumping into Carmen's lap.

When the show ended, Jamal, Carmen, and Mia made their way to one of the mobile concession stands at the park. They purchased hot dogs, chips, and sodas, and found a spot in the picnic area to enjoy their meal. Mia's eyes lit up as she bit into her hot dog, ketchup and mustard smeared across her face.

After they finished eating, Jamal pulled out a kite from his backpack. It was a pretty princess kite, with pink and purple streamers trailing behind it. Mia's eyes widened in excitement as Jamal handed it to her.

"You want to fly it?" he asked, smiling.

Mia nodded eagerly, and Jamal helped her hold the kite as he unraveled the string. Once it was ready, he handed the string to Mia and showed her how to run with the kite to get it in the air.

Mia took off running, laughing as the kite soared higher and higher. Carmen watched with a smile, grateful for Jamal's kindness and patience with her daughter. She couldn't help but feel a little guilty for not trusting him enough to let him pick her up at her house earlier on in their friendship. But today, he picked her and Mia up for the first time. They were outside watering flowers when he'd come to pick them up for the show.

When Mia finally tired of running, Jamal took over flying the kite while Carmen and Mia sat on a nearby bench. Mia leaned against her mother, her eyes heavy with exhaustion.

"You had a lot of fun today, didn't you?" Carmen asked, stroking Mia's hair.

Mia nodded sleepily, her eyes fluttering closed.

"I think it's time to head home," Jamal said, looking at his watch.

Carmen nodded, and they packed up their things. Jamal carried Mia to his car, and she was asleep before they even pulled out of the parking lot.

As they drove, Carmen felt a twinge of nervousness. It was going to be the first time Jamal would see the inside of her house, and she knew it wasn't much to look at. She had been slowly trying to acquire furniture, but it was a slow process. She was more comfortable with him seeing the inside of her place now that she at least had a real bed, sofa, and breakfast table now.

When they pulled up to her house, Jamal brought their stuff in as Carmen carried Mia inside and lay her down on the toddler bed in Mia's room. He looked around the small living room, taking in the sparse furnishings.

"It's not much," Carmen said, feeling embarrassed.

"It's cozy," Jamal replied, smiling. "And it's yours."

Carmen smiled back, feeling less self-conscious due to Jamal's understanding and support.

As Mia slumbered peacefully in her room, Carmen and Jamal settled onto the couch in the living room. The day's events had left them both in high spirits, and Carmen felt even more drawn to the man beside her.

"Thank you again for today, Jamal. Mia had such a wonderful time."

"It was my pleasure. I love spending time with you both." He paused, then added, "You know, now that

I've seen your place, maybe you'd like to come over to mine for dinner one evening?"

"Umm... I guess that's fair," she replied, uncertain. She wanted to be careful not to lead Jamal on, especially given her complicated situation with Tony.

A moment of silence stretched between them, heavy with unspoken thoughts. Jamal broke it, his gaze traveling over Carmen's form. "You look very lovely in that outfit. Orange looks really good with your skin tone."

"Well, thank you so much, Mr. Adams."

"You're welcome, Señorita Diaz."

As Jamal's stare deepened, his chestnut eyes locked onto Carmen's, the doorbell suddenly rang, shattering the moment.

"Were you expecting someone?" Jamal asked, surprise evident in his tone.

Carmen shook her head, equally puzzled. "No."

They both rose from the couch, Jamal following Carmen to the door. As she opened it, Tony's face came into view, causing Carmen's heart to floor.

"Tony, what are you doing here?" Carmen asked, stricken with confusion and panic.

Tony's eyes shifted between Carmen and Jamal, with something unreadable passing over his expression. Without waiting for an invitation, he brushed past Carmen and strode into the living room.

"I was off and wanted to surprise Mia and you."

"Me?" she echoed, acutely aware of Jamal's presence behind her. She silently prayed that Jamal wouldn't misinterpret the situation.

Tony took a seat on the couch, sinking into the sparsely stuffed cushions. Carmen was becoming very anxious, hoping against hope that Tony wouldn't be crazy and jealous enough to reveal their intimate encounters to Jamal out of spite.

"Mia's asleep," Carmen said quickly, to get Tony to leave before any awkwardness or confrontation arose.

Tony shrugged nonchalantly. "I came all this way, I'll wait."

Jamal sniggered. "Man, you came unannounced, obviously, and Carmen has company."

"I'm family," Tony retorted, rising from the couch and closing the distance between himself and Jamal, as if challenging him. "I'm her daughter's father."

Jamal felt a rush of adrenaline course through his veins, his body tensing instinctively at the perceived threat. Although Tony was a bit chunkier, Jamal was a few inches taller and more muscular. He knew he could pulverize Tony if it came to that, but he didn't want to upset Carmen.

"Of course," Jamal conceded, calming down.

Tony's eyes narrowed, and he opened his mouth as if to say something further, but Jamal cut him off. "Maybe I should just...go."

"Don't leave on my account," Tony said, a hint of smugness in his voice. "Besides, if you're in my baby's life, I should get to know you."

Jamal glanced at Carmen, unsure of how to proceed. He couldn't tell by her expression what she was thinking or felt about the situation.

"That's respectable," Jamal agreed, deciding to take the high road.

Carmen took a deep breath, attempting to regain control of the situation. "Why don't we all have a seat, and I'll fix us something to drink?"

As the two men complied, Carmen surveyed her kitchen. She realized she didn't have much to offer in terms of refreshments. Luckily, she did have exactly two sodas left in the fridge. She fixed herself a glass of water from the tap, chilling it with ice from the tray in the freezer.

When Carmen returned with the drinks, she sat between Tony and Jamal, creating a physical barrier between the two men. You could totally feel the agitation in the room, and Carmen was freaking out as she tried to manage the delicate situation.

Tony 's eyes were fixed on Jamal. "So, what was your name again?"

"Jamal-Jamal Adams."

"How and when did you two meet?"

Before Jamal could respond, Carmen jumped in, "Oh, he helped me one evening when my car battery went dead ..."

Jamal took mental note of Carmen's abrupt interjection and her apparent reluctance to provide a specific timeline. He tried to convince himself that he was reading too much into it, attributing her behavior to nervousness caused by the earlier tension between him and Tony.

"What do you do for a living, and you got kids?"

"I'm an accountant, and no, I don't."

Tony smirked. "Aww, that explains a lot. That's why you don't understand this dynamic."

With a manipulative glint in his eye, Tony proceeded to tell Jamal that he would always be a part of Carmen's life because of Mia. As Tony spoke, Jamal couldn't help but recall the warnings his parents, particularly his father, had given him about the drama of dating women with children and dealing with their baby daddies.

Jamal sipped his soda, trying to maintain his composure. "Of course, but the involvement should be limited."

"No, I don't agree. We're a family," Tony retorted.

"Yes, for the sake of Mia, he just means we will always be cordial with one another."

"Please, don't speak for me, Car."

Carmen fell silent, chastened by Tony's rebuke. Jamal was about to speak when Mia suddenly appeared, rubbing her eyes sleepily. Upon seeing Tony, she exclaimed, "Daddy!" and ran to him.

Jamal stood up, sensing it was time for him to leave. "I'll see you around," he told Carmen as he headed for the door.

"Jamal, I'll call you..." Carmen called out desperately as he walked to his car.

Tony smirked at the scene of Jamal leaving angrily, hugging Mia tightly. He turned to Carmen, his eyes roving over her body. "You look real nice, Car."

As the door closed behind Jamal, trepidation suddenly hit Carmen. She worried that she might lose Jamal because of this complicated situation with Tony.

Chapter 10

Recipe for Drama

Jamal Adams

Jamal sat behind his desk at work, reviewing figures for the dry cleaning owner's account. He'd finally figured out where the man's wife had gone wrong with her figures. Taking a mental break, he stared out of his office window. Two squirrels played on the balcony below him, having obviously jumped off a nearby tree. His thoughts drifted to Carmen and all the time they'd spent together recently.

As if he'd conjured her up, his phone rang with Carmen's name flashing on the screen.

"Hi Carmen," he answered. "How's your day?"

"I'm good," she replied, anxious. Without preamble, she launched into an apology about Tony showing up after their park outing on Saturday.

"You already called and apologized Sunday. You don't have to apologize every time we engage in conversation. We're good, relax."

Carmen persisted, trying to make it right. Her words tumbled out, filled with remorse and explanations.

"Look," Jamal interrupted. "Yes, it was uncomfortable, but he's Mia's father and that's never going to change. So, as long as I'm in your life, and I want to be, then I have to get used to dealing with him."

Carmen exhaled in relief. She switched to more upbeat conversation, expressing gratitude for Jamal's being so understanding . They chatted cheerfully for a minute, but beneath Jamal's pleasant demeanor, his true feelings remained unexpressed. As they said their goodbyes and hung up, Jamal's smile faded, replaced by a furrowed brow as he contemplated the complexities of his relationship with Carmen.

Tavaris leaned against the doorframe of Jamal's office, with concern. He'd overheard the tail end of Jamal's conversation with Carmen, and the worry lines on his friend's face spoke volumes.

"You good, man?" Tavaris asked, stepping into the room.

Jamal looked up, surprised. "T, didn't see you there. Yeah, I'm fine."

Tavaris shook his head, unconvinced. "Nah, I heard that call. Sounds like Carmen's got some complicated stuff going on."

"It's not that bad, really. Just her ex showing up unexpectedly."

"That's exactly what I'm talking about. Her ex popping up whenever he feels like it? That's a recipe for drama, bro."

"Look, I don't want to overstep, but have you thought about the possibility that Tony might be trying to maneuver his way back into Carmen's life? Or even her bed?"

"I'd be lying if I said the thought hadn't crossed my mind. But Carmen seems pretty adamant about keeping things strictly co-parental with him."

"I hear you, man, but exes have a way of complicating things. Especially when there's a kid involved. Tony could be using Mia as an excuse to worm his way back in."

Jamal considered Tavaris's words. He knew his friend meant well, but the thought of Tony trying to manipulate his way back into Carmen's life left a bitter taste in his mouth.

"Carmen's not naive. She's been through enough with that guy to know better than to let him back in like that."

Tavaris held up his hands in a placating gesture. "I'm not saying she is, bro. But Tony seems like the type who doesn't take 'no' for an answer. Those are the charming and manipulative ones."

Jamal couldn't argue with that assessment. He'd witnessed Tony firsthand this past weekend. The thought of him using those tactics on Carmen made Jamal pissed.

"Maybe I'm just being paranoid," Tavaris conceded. "But I know how much you care about this Carmen and her kid. I don't want to see you get hurt if Tony tries to pull some shady moves."

Jamal appreciated his friend's concern, even if he didn't want to admit the possibility of Tony's ulterior motives. He knew Tavaris was looking out for him, and that meant more than he could express but he wanted to believe there was nothing to worry about and that he could trust Carmen around Tony.

"I hear you, T," Jamal said, offering a small smile. "And I appreciate you watching my back. It's not like that. Tony's Mia's father. He has a right to see his daughter."

"Sure, but does he have the right to mess with your relationship?" Tavaris countered. "Seems like he's causing problems."

"You don't know the whole situation."

"Maybe not, but I know you. And I see how this is affecting you."

The two friends went back and forth, Jamal staunchly defending Carmen and the situation, while Tavaris voiced his concerns. Their debate grew heated, each man's perspective clashing with the other's. Finally they calmed back down.

"Look, J. I'm just looking out for you. I don't want to see you get hurt again."

"I appreciate that, T. But Carmen's worth it. She and Mia both are."

Tavaris nodded, understanding but still unconvinced. "Just be careful, alright? Drama has a way of snowballing.

"All I'm saying is even if you trust her, you know how men are because you are one. He can't be trusted coming around her all times a day, alone."

Jamal's patience was wearing thin. "I'm sure Carmen has boundaries and has the situation under control," he stated, his tone leaving no room for argument.

"Hey, you even said once that your folks didn't think this chick was the right choice. All I'm saying is, just keep your eyes open my man, that's all." With that, Tavaris left the office, leaving Jamal alone with his thoughts.

As the door closed behind Tavaris, Jamal leaned back in his chair, his mind a whirlwind of conflicting emotions. He wanted to believe that Carmen was a woman he could trust, a woman who needed him. She was beautiful, kind, appreciative, virtuous, a good mother. She was everything he'd been looking for in a woman.

Yet, Tavaris' words echoed in his head, along with the doubts his parents had expressed. The memory of his mother's concerned face and his father's disapproving frown flashed through his mind. They had worried about the complications that came with dating a single mother, especially one with such recent baggage.

But as Jamal gazed out the window, and thought about how he felt when he's with Carmen, he felt sure that it was meant to be. Despite the warnings from Tavaris and the reservations of his parents, Jamal was resolved to pursue a relationship with Carmen. He believed in her, in the connection they shared, and in the potential for a future together.

Chapter 11

Night Out With the Girls

Carmen Diaz

Situated in the vibrant downtown core of Atlanta, the nightclub pulsated with energy, music and vibrant lights. The atmosphere was permeated by the fragrance of perfumes, colognes, and a subtle trace of perspiration. Bass throbbed incessantly, reverberating across the packed dance floor, where bodies twisted and gyrated in a chaotic dance.

Carmen sat at the table, absentmindedly stirring her drink, staring towards the dance floor as the bass vibrated through her chest, enhancing the nervous jitters she was experiencing. She watched as Felicia and Lola laughed and chatted, their faces glowing in the dim neon lighting.

Felicia was stunning, her long braids accentuating her flawless mocha skin and full lips. The lavender bodysuit she wore hugged every curve, the deep v-neck showing off her sizeable cleavage. Lola was equally radiant, her petite frame sheathed in a sultry red dress that stopped mid-thigh. Her chestnut curls cascaded over her bare shoulders, framing the gleam of risqué in her eyes.

In contrast, Carmen felt plain. She fussed with the hem of her knee-length black skirt, tugging at the red blouse she had chosen for the night out. The conservative outfit made her feel like she was going to a job interview rather than a nightclub with her best friends. But she had chosen the outfit intentionally, hoping it would serve as a male repellent.

As another man's eyes roamed over Lola, she shot him a withering glare. Carmen couldn't help but smile. Lola always commanded respect, no matter the situation or setting. Her fiery spirit was not to be trifled with.

The crowd on the dance floor continued to sway and pulse to the music. Strobe lights flickered, giving the club an ethereal glow. Servers wove their way through the throngs of people, delivering drinks that sloshed precariously. The vibe was intense. Carmen took a deep breath, soaking it all in. It had been too long since she had felt this free, this unburdened. For a few hours, she could forget about her responsibilities and just be. This night was exactly what she needed.

The friends ordered another round of drinks. Lola requested a martini, Felicia a white wine, and Carmen decided to be the more responsible one and order another mocktail. The waiter smiled rather flirtatiously at Carmen.

"Ah shit, looks like he was feelin' you girl," Felicia teased, wiggling her eyebrows suggestively.

"Yeah, prima. You might want to drop those digits too. That waiter was fine-fine," Lola chimed in with a smirk.

"I'm not looking for a man right now," Carmen responded, gazing around the club at single men of all ages hitting on women in their 20s and early 30s. "What did that song just say?"

"Car, you are so green nowadays. Mommy-hood is making you lame," Felicia laughed.

"Naw, I think I'm just maturing." Carmen shrugged.

"Look, loosen up Car. Have some fun, leave your worries behind and live a little tonight. You might even get lucky." Felicia nudged her suggestively.

"I'm not going home with some guy I meet at a club." Carmen shook her head firmly.

"No silly, but you can exchange numbers though."

The waiter came back with the drinks and casually left his card on the table near Carmen before walking off. He was a freelance photographer as well. Carmen wasn't interested and slid the card to Lola who quickly pursed it.

"You're gonna really call that waiter?"

"Heck yeah, did you not see those biceps prima?" Lola replied with a grin.

The three friends dissolved into laughter. As their mirth subsided, the conversation turned to more serious matters.

"So how's things with that trouble maker at your job?" Carmen inquired, looking at Lola .

"Don't even get me started. I wanted to slap that bitch sideways yesterday."

"What'd she do?"

Lola launched into a tirade, listing the opportunist's latest offenses - the credit stealing, the passive aggressive comments, the blatant disrespect. Carmen and Felicia listened intently, making sympathetic noises.

When Lola finally finished her rant, the topic shifted to Carmen's love life. She insisted Jamal was just a good friend, but the way she described his kindness and support made her true feelings evident.

"Girl, we've seen the pics you've texted us of him. That man is fine as hell and obviously cares about you," Felicia asserted. "You need to move on from Tony and give Jamal a real chance."

"I have moved on from Tony."

"Not if you're still fucking him. And that arrangement is pretty foul, cuz."

Felicia nodded emphatically. "Yeah, that's wrong as hell what he's doing. He's a piece of shit, Car."

Carmen sighed, staring down into her drink. She knew her friends were right. She deserved more than the dysfunctional arrangement she had settled into with Tony.

"You're absolutely right," she said finally, looking up at Felicia and Lola's concerned faces. "I need to stop sleeping with Tony for money. It's not healthy for me or Mia."

Felicia nodded, reaching out to squeeze Carmen's hand . "You know we've got your back, right? "

"I know. Thank you." She was grateful for her friends, but the thought of finally cutting ties with Tony made her anxious.

Lola seemed to sense Carmen's trepidation. "Look, it's not gonna be easy," she said bluntly. "Tony's a selfish asshole who's used to taking advantage. But you gotta stand up for yourself and Mia now."

"You're right. I need to be strong and do what's best for both of us."

"Exactly!" Felicia exclaimed. "No more late night booty calls in exchange for grocery money. File for child support and let the courts deal with that dead-beat."

Despite the gravity of the conversation, Carmen couldn't help but chuckle at Felicia's bluntness. Her friends always had a way of putting things into perspective.

Interrupting their conversation, a guy with long locs approached their table with his eyes fixed on Lola. He exuded confidence as he leaned in, flashing a charming smile.

"Hey beautiful, can I buy you a drink?"

Lola's eyes roamed over him, a coy grin playing on her lips. She was clearly intrigued, but not ready to make it easy for him.

"Thanks, but I'm good," she replied, her tone playful.

Undeterred, he extended his hand. "How about a dance then?"

Lola's grin widened as she took his hand, allowing him to lead her to the dance floor.

As they walked away, Felicia turned back to Carmen, her expression growing serious. "Look, Car, you need to put Tony on child support. It'll take the pressure off you financially and emotionally."

Carmen sighed, swirling her mocktail. "I know, but – "

"No buts," Felicia cut in. "You won't have to beg him for money anymore, and you definitely won't feel pressured into sex. That's terrible how he's treating you. You don't deserve that kind of treatment. No woman does."

"I know. I put up with it because I didn't want to put Mia's father in the system. He hasn't exactly had a stable job record. Men that can't hold jobs... child support tends to mess them up in so many ways."

Felicia shook her head firmly. "That's not your problem, Car. Just like keeping his pecker wet isn't your problem. It's his."

She stood up abruptly, grabbing Carmen's hand. "Now, get on this floor and dance with me."

As Felicia pulled her towards the dance floor, Carmen caught sight of Lola twerking with the dreaded hunk. The bass pulsed through her body as she began to move, her mind whirling with thoughts of Tony and child support.

While she danced, Carmen seriously considered what Felicia had said about filing for child support. The idea of freedom from Tony's manipulation was tempting, but the potential consequences for him weighed heavily on her mind.

Chapter 12

Mesmerizing

Carmen Diaz

Carmen's heart raced as she stepped into the opulent restaurant, acutely aware of Jamal's gaze following her every move. The rose-pink dress highlighted everything he loved about her shape, and she felt a mix of confidence and nervousness under his appreciative stare.

Jamal couldn't tear his eyes away from Carmen. Her beauty was mesmerizing, and he found himself struggling to focus on anything else. As they were led to their table, he watched the subtle sway of her hips, captivated by her grace and quiet allure.

The restaurant's ambiance was intoxicating. Soft, reddish light bathed the room in a warm glow, while the twinkling lights of Atlanta stretched out before them through the floor-to-ceiling windows. The artificial candles on each table added to the romantic atmosphere magnificently.

After helping Carmen into her seat, Jamal took his place across from her. Their eyes locked, and for a moment, the bustling restaurant faded away. Carmen's lips, painted a nude pink, curved into a shy smile, and Jamal felt his pulse rise.

As they perused the menus, Jamal's gaze occasionally drifted to Carmen's décolletage, accentuated by the strapless neckline of her dress. He quickly averted his eyes, not wanting to be caught staring, but found it increasingly difficult to concentrate on the menu before him.

The city skyline provided a stunning backdrop to their dinner, but neither Carmen nor Jamal paid it much attention. They were far too engrossed in each other, stealing glances and sharing soft smiles as they waited for the server to arrive.

"So, how has your week been going at the pharmacy?"

"It's been going pretty well. Just wish these people would not come inside who suspect they have Covid. We have a testing tent outside for that, and the sign is easy to spot."

Jamal's forehead crinkled . "You're not contagious are you?"

"Oh, not at all," Carmen reassured him quickly. "I wouldn't be here if I were."

Their conversation was interrupted by the arrival of the server, a man who exuded an air of sophistication that seemed almost out of place. He carried himself with such poise that both Carmen and Jamal found themselves momentarily distracted, imagining him more suited to serving royalty than patrons in an Atlanta restaurant.

"Are you all ready to order?" the server inquired, his crisp accent adding to his regal demeanor.

Jamal pulled his attention back to the menu. "We'd like to start with an appetizer." He proceeded to order a selection of dishes for them to share, along with a bottle of red wine.

As the server collected their menus, his gaze lingered on Carmen for a moment longer than necessary, a faint blush coloring his cheeks as he turned to leave.

"You catch that?" Jamal's lips quirked into a grin.

"Yeah, but I have a strong feeling he's more into you than me," Carmen giggled.

"Thanks for bringing me here. This place is lov ely... so elegant," Carmen said, her gaze sweeping across the polished decor.

"Very fitting then. You're elegant, Car. And beautiful and sexy, if you don't mind me saying that."

Carmen blushed. They were supposed to be just friends, yet the chemistry between them simmered beneath the surface, undeniable and fiery, like a volcano waiting to erupt. Anyone who took her to an expensive place like this had to see her as more than just a friend. She couldn't help but admire him as well—his gray suit tailored to perfection, his fresh haircut accentuating his strong jawline. The way his beard glistened in the dim light sent a thrill down her spine.

"I don't mind," she replied, a playful lilt in her voice. "You look very eye-catching yourself tonight, as a matter of fact."

"Do I?" he asked, feigning surprise while a smile crept across his lips.

"Oh yes, you do." Carmen leaned slightly forward, feeling bold under the spell of his cologne and his alluring chestnut eyes .

"Well, good. I tried." Jamal's grin widened. "These candles are a whole mood, aren't they?"

"They're perfect," Carmen agreed, admiring the flickering flames that danced between them.

Just then, the server glided over with an air of professionalism that seemed almost rehearsed. He placed a polished tray on their table and carefully arranged the dishes before them.

“Bon appétit,” he said with a flourish before stepping aside.

Carmen’s eyes lit up at the sight of their appetizers: delicate escargots nestled in buttery garlic sauce surrounded by crusty bread for dipping; rich duck pâté presented on a wooden board alongside tangy cornichons; and crispy onion tarts that exuded warmth and savory aromas.

"Wow," she breathed in awe, taking in the artistry of each dish.

Jamal chuckled softly as he lifted an escargot from its shell with his fork. "Care for some?"

"Only if you promise not to laugh when I try it." Her laughter rang out like music in the refined atmosphere.

“Deal,” he replied playfully before popping the escargot into his mouth. A satisfied expression crossed his face as he savored it.

Carmen followed suit hesitantly but found herself delightfully surprised by the burst of flavor that exploded on her palate. "Okay... not bad at all," she admitted, nodding appreciatively.

As they savored their appetizers, the conversation between Carmen and Jamal deepened. The months they'd spent together had cultivated a connection that went beyond mere friendship, and both felt the need to address it.

Jamal, his eyes fixed on Carmen's, spoke with conviction. "I've really enjoyed our time together, Car. I want you to know that I see you as more than just a friend. I'd like to keep seeing you in settings like this."

Carmen's heart fluttered like a delicate butterfly as his words echoed through her ears. The scent of his cologne imbued the space, adding an intoxicating layer to the moment. She felt the same pull towards him, but the scars from her past held her back. "I feel the same way, Jamal. But I need more time to heal, to trust my judgment again."

"Do you trust me?"

Before Carmen could answer, the server appeared, interrupting their moment to clear away the empty appetizer plates. "Are you ready for the main course?"

After placing their orders, the server left, and Jamal sat his gaze on Carmen, waiting for her to answer his earlier question. Carmen took a deep breath, gathering her thoughts.

"I do trust you, Jamal," she began, her voice faint. "But I'm not ready for a full-blown relationship yet. There's just so much going on in my life right now."

Carmen's mind was overwhelmed with reasons for her inability to fully commit- her financial struggles, Tony's persistent control issues, not to mention that her parents wouldn't approve of her being with Jamal, regardless of how great he was. But, she didn't want to share all those details with him.

The silence stretched between them, broken only by the arrival of their main course. They began to eat, the awkwardness dissipating as they focused on their meals and sipped their wine. Carmen found herself drinking a bit more heavily than usual, using the glass as a shield to avoid Jamal's gaze.

Jamal felt as if he had made some headway though. At least now, he knew she was attracted, that she had some feelings. He just needed to help her let her guard down a bit. The way she was drinking, it looked to him as if she would be doing just that, very soon.

During the drive home, their conversation primarily revolved around the delectable cuisine at the restaurant. Carmen, her inhibitions lowered by the wine, gushed about the restaurant's ambiance.

"The chandeliers were just breathtaking." Her words were slightly slurred. "And those little candles on the tables? So romantic."

The three glasses of wine she consumed were doing their job. Jamal smiled, his own mind clear. He only had two, but it didn't really faze him since he's used to having a glass of red wine occasionally during the week.

When they arrived at Carmen's tiny home, Jamal escorted her to the door. As Carmen held her keys to unlock the door, she turned to thank him one last time. In that moment, Jamal seized the opportunity. His hand found the small of her back, pulling her close. Their eyes locked, a silent exchange of desire, before Jamal's lips claimed hers in a long intense kiss.

Carmen's body responded instantly. She felt a rush of heat between her legs, her panties growing damp with arousal. Pressed against her, she could feel Jamal's manhood hardening, through their clothing. It was so...huge.

The intensity of the moment threatened to overwhelm Carmen. Every fiber of her being screamed for more, urging her to invite him inside, to give in to the passion that had been building between them. But a small voice of reason cut through the fog of desire.

With great reluctance, Carmen broke the kiss. She stood there, panting, her chest heaving as she struggled to catch her breath in the cool March night air.

"Why'd we stop?" Jamal asked, breathy.

"What do you mean, we're outside," Carmen replied, though her body ached to continue.

A blush crept across Jamal's face as he ventured, "Do you want to go inside?"

Carmen wanted nothing more than to say yes, to lead him to her bedroom and lose herself with him. But she hesitated, torn between desire and caution.

"I..." she began, before placing a chaste kiss on his cheek. "Thank you for a beautiful evening."

With a small wave, Carmen retreated into her home, leaving Jamal standing on the porch. As she closed the door behind her, she leaned against it, her body still yearning with unfulfilled desire, her panties wetter than she could ever remember them being. As she reached her hand underneath her dress, she could feel the dampness seeping through the fabric of her panties. The sound of her own quickened breaths filled her ears. She couldn't help but shiver, a tingling sensation spreading across her skin, as she realized just how aroused she truly was.

Chapter 13

Come Back Home

Carmen Diaz

Carmen stood in her bedroom with the door cracked, holding the phone to her ear and glancing into the living room to keep an eye on Mia playing in the playpen. Her brows knitted together in a frown as she listened to Tony declaim his point of view .

"I told you, I didn't have enough hours this past week. You know I'm living paycheck to paycheck." Carmen explained, her tone overflowing with an unmistakable sense of frustration.

"Shit, you always hounding me for money, Car. Bring your ass back home, and we can afford to live a decent life. Didn't we before?" Tony spoke impatiently.

"Barely."

"That's 'cause I was working part-time. But since they hired me on permanent at the warehouse, I get more hours and am even eligible for benefits."

"Great, so help me out!" Carmen's voice got louder, showing how desperate she was.

"I have my own rent, groceries, car note, insurance and shit to pay for. I can't afford two fuckin' households, Car. Get off that niggah's dick and come back home."

As she listened to his words, Carmen's eyes bulged and she could feel anger seething inside her. "Seriously? You're going there? Jamal and I are just friends."

"I may not have a high school diploma, but I got freakin' common sense, and either your ass is fuckin' him or he's tryin' to fuck. I see how he looks at you," Tony insisted.

Carmen paused, with a tinge of uncertainty. She thought about the night with Jamal at the elegant restaurant, the park concert, museum, and all the other times they'd spent together. A part of her really did want to know what Tony saw, if Jamal truly cared about her, wanted her, desired her. Because she sure as hell wanted him. But the rational part of her mind knew better than to entertain Tony's accusations.

"And how's that?" Carmen barley voiced.

"You'd really love to know, wouldn't you? What about what's best for Mia?"

"I'm always doing what's best for my daughter."

"Our daughter," Tony corrected her, his tone sharp. "And if that were true, you'd bring your ass back home and give our little girl a whole damn family instead of trying to be this feminist independent woman type shit."

Mia's agitation grew in her playpen as she accidentally tossed her stuffed rabbit out, her whimpers threatening to turn into full-blown cries.

"Tony...I gotta go. Are you helping me or not?"

"I ain't got it, Car. Didn't I freakin' explain that already? You're short, I'm short. If you'd come home, we'd have more than enough. This shit is on you. Choose between the Mandingo or your family." With that, Tony clicked off the call in anger.

Carmen breathed out slowly; overwhelmed by her financial issues and Tony's accusations. She made her way to Mia's playpen, scooping up the stuffed rabbit and handing it back to her daughter. Mia's tears subsided as she clutched the toy, and Carmen sat down beside her, engaging in playtime with games and toddler puzzles.

Jamal was coming over later anyway for dinner, she figured she'd just have to ask him if she could borrow a couple of hundred until next month. She wasn't exactly comfortable with doing this. But at this point, she felt that there was no other choice.

When it was time to prepare dinner, Carmen busied herself in the kitchen. A blend of herbs and spices was used to season the chicken, creating a fragrant smell that consumed her small house. As the chicken baked in the oven, she prepared a side of rice and beans, a favorite dish of her childhood. The meal was finished with a simple green salad, and Carmen nervously set the table for three, anticipating Jamal's arrival.

Before she knew it, Jamal was knocking at her door. When she opened it, he had a humongous gift bag with him.

"What's all this?" Carmen asked, eyes growing big.

"I haven't done anything special for my pal Mia in a while."

"Mal!" Mia ran to Jamal, her little arms outstretched.

Carmen took the gift bag as Jamal lifted Mia high in the air.

"Fly me high!" she shouted in laughter.

Carmen admired how great he was with Mia. Watching him with her made her feel as if he'd make a great step dad.

They sat and ate, conversation flowing easily between them. Jamal talked a lot about Mr. Johnson. You could tell the man was a real work.

"Oh my goodness, that man really gets on my last nerves complaining about his wife," Jamal told her, shaking his head.

"Is he that bad?"

"Listening to him, you'd swear she was trying to sabotage his business. But, the truth is, he's just frugal and she buys what's needed, not always telling him about all the purchases up front."

"Wow! That's nuts," giggled Carmen. "It's like they're making you a marriage counselor."

"I feel like it at times," he expressed, a wry smile on his face.

Mia sat there eating, alternating between her spoon and chunky little fingers, unconcerned with the adult conversation around her. Jamal smiled at her and then back at Carmen.

"You're a great mom. That's one reason I think I like you so much."

Carmen blushed. "Really? Most men don't like baby mamas, according to the internet."

"That's most men," Jamal admitted. "But not *this* man. I get to see what kind of mother you'd be by watching you with Mia."

Carmen's forehead wrinkled slightly. "What kind of mother I'd be?"

Jamal smiled, not wanting to say that he meant what type of mom she'd be with their child together. There was an unspoken but undeniable significance to his words.

Carmen contemplated how to broach the subject of borrowing money for her car payment. The opportunity seemed to slip away with each passing moment, and she found herself growing increasingly anxious.

After dinner, Mia's eyes grew huge as she unwrapped Jamal's gift. It was a giant stuffed rabbit.

"Wow! He's as big as you, Mia," Carmen smiled.

"Thanks so much, Jamal." Without hesitation, she planted a soft kiss on his cheek.

He grabbed her arm as she was about to walk away, pulling her into a hug. His body touching hers caused a shiver to run down her spine.

"Anything for you guys," he murmured, his breath tickling her ear. "I'm just showing my commitment to both of you. You and Mia come as a pair. I get that, Car."

Carmen was touched by his words, realizing the depth of his feelings. She instructed Mia to thank Jamal, and she happily did so.

"Tank you, Mal," Mia babbled, her tiny arms wrapping around Jamal's legs.

After playing with stuffed animals a few minutes, they all watched cartoons together. Mia soon dozed off in Carmen's lap. Carmen took Mia to her room and laid her down.

Returning to the living room, Carmen joined Jamal on the couch and switched to Netflix. As a passionate kiss played out on screen, a nervous giggle escaped her lips. Jamal turned to her, a mischievous glint in his eye. He smiled and grabbed her chin, turning her face towards him. He kissed her, prolonging the grip on her bottom lip. Carmen's panties irrigated with desire.

Jamal's hand slid up her back, fingers prancing along her spine before curling around the hem of her shirt. With a gentle tug, he pulled it upward, exposing her soft golden tinted skin . Carmen shivered at the sensation but didn't pull away; instead, she leaned into him, craving more.

As Jamal's fingers brushed against the fabric of her bra, he squeezed her breast softly, eliciting a gasp from Carmen. She felt alive—desirable in a way she hadn't in ages. In that moment, everything outside ceased to exist.

Mia's soft snores from down the hall were drowned out by the quickening breaths between them. The kiss intensified as Carmen found herself straddling Jamal's waist, her body fitting perfectly against him. A flame coursed through her veins; she was ready to let go of everything—the worries about Tony, finances, and being a single mom, even if just for tonight.

But as Jamal's hands explored further beneath her shirt and his lips pushed harder against hers, something within Carmen hesitated. Clarity hit like a cold splash of water.

"Wait," she breathed out softly against his mouth.

Jamal paused mid-kiss, his hand cupping her breast as he searched her eyes for understanding. “What’s wrong?” His voice dropped an octave; concerned.

Carmen’s emotions were all over the place. She wanted Jamal so bad her head was spinning. And she cared for him deeply, appreciating how well he treated Mia like his own. But could she really take this step?

“Not like this,” she said finally, lifting herself off him despite how hard it was.

He released his hold on her and ran a hand along his beard, breathing heavily as he leaned back slightly to give them both space.

“I get it,” he replied quietly but didn’t mask the disappointment in his gaze.

Intense and precarious, the moment lingered as they both reflected on what had almost happened.

Jamal expressed to Carmen how much he cared for her and he let her know that it was becoming more difficult for him to be 'just friends' with her. His confession wasn't entirely unexpected, but hearing it aloud made it real—tangible. She could see the intensity in his eyes, the way his body tensed as he spoke, betraying the depth of his feelings.

"I'm too attracted to you to suppress it any longer. Every time I'm around you, my body responds." Jamal admitted.

Her own body was responding to his words and proximity. Carmen understood exactly what he meant. She felt it too, that flame that seemed to ignite between them whenever they were close.

"What I'm saying Carmen is, soon you're going to have to make a decision. If it's just staying friends, we have to have some distance between us. We can't see each other as much."

The thought of seeing Jamal less often wasn't even something Carmen wanted to consider. She'd grown accustomed to his presence, his support, the way he made her feel—wanted, appreciated, understood. But she also recognized the fairness in his request. It wasn't right to keep him in limbo, especially when her own feelings were so complex.

"I understand. I just need a little more time, please give me that," Carmen pleaded softly.

Jamal nodded. "Okay."

With that, he left, and Carmen closed the door behind him. The silence in the apartment felt oppressive now, as she leaned against the door. Her thoughts began to tumble over one another.

She thought about the money she hadn't asked for, to pay the car note. She thought about the decision she now had to make, one that would impact not just her life but Mia's as well. How would Tony react if she got involved with Jamal romantically? What about her parents?

She didn't know what to do. But amidst all these practical concerns, her body erupted with a different kind of energy. She couldn't deny the effect Jamal had on her—the way her skin tingled at his touch, how her breath caught when he looked at her with those intense eyes. All she knew was that dark skinned gorgeous man made her soil her panties every time he even breathed her way. His smell, the hue of his skin, the heat of his body, and the lump in his crouch. It was so huge when she straddled his waist.

Overwhelmed by desire and confusion, Carmen walked to her room, pulled her vibrator out of her dresser drawer and exhaled. Remembering straddling him on the couch earlier incited her juices to stir again. She knew that while this might provide temporary relief, the bigger decisions still awaited her.

Chapter 14

A Difficult Conversation

Carmen Diaz

Spring was in the air, and it was time for blooms. Carmen was blooming too, evolving. She was taking charge. She was filing for child support, just like the other dozen women sitting in the DCSS office that morning. Carmen's fingers tapped nervously on her knee as she waited for her name to be called.

"Ms. Diaz," a voice finally announced.

Carmen stood, pulled in a deep breath, and followed the clerk to a small, windowless office. The man behind the desk, middle-aged with thinning hair, went over her paperwork methodically. He explained the process, in a monotone that belied the significance of his words.

"So, I don't need to do anything else for now?"

The clerk looked up from the papers. "We'll let you know if we need any more information from you. For now, this needs to be processed and after we can serve Mr. Antonio Lopez."

At the mention of Tony's full name, Carmen felt even more guilt than she'd anticipated. For some reason those words didn't make Carmen feel as happy as they should have. All she could do was see Tony possibly losing his license or his freedom if he couldn't pay on time. A man who had limited skills and no high-school diploma. She wanted Mia to be provided for, but she felt guilty doing this to Tony. Felicia told her not to feel guilty though-that it was Tony's problem.

"You're doing what's best for Mia," she murmured too low for the clerk to comprehend.

Pushing aside her conflicting emotions, Carmen managed a subtle smile. "Thank you, Sir," she said, rising from her chair to leave.

•••••••••••

Carmen painted on her most convincing smile as her mother opened the door to let her in. Dinner at her parents, she had been avoiding it for months. She needed them to think she was doing well.

"Where's Mia? We thought we'd see Mia too," her mother fussed, as the cat appeared out of nowhere.

"She's at Tony's mom's."

"She sees his mom, but not your mom?"

"Mama...it's not like that. She asked. And she volunteered to keep her a few evenings this coming week while I work overtime. Besides, you guys see Mia often."

"It's been a while Carmen," Maria responded. "Besides, it can never be too often," she expressed.

Carmen nodded, not wanting to get into an argument. She followed her mother into the cozy kitchen where the scent of simmering frijoles pervaded the room.

Carmen took a seat at the small kitchen table as her mother busied herself at the stove.

"How is Tony doing?" her mother asked, glancing over her shoulder. "We haven't seen him in awhile."

Carmen shifted in her seat, weighing her words carefully. "He's good. Busy with work lately."

It wasn't exactly a lie, he was full time and working a permanent job now. Carmen stirred the conversation to safer topics until her father's voice boomed from the living room, calling for her.

"There's my girl!" he said as Carmen entered. She crossed the room to give him a quick hug before sitting on the sofa.

"Sorry I'm late, Papá. Traffic was backed up something awful on 85." Another harmless fib. Her father nodded, none the wiser as the cat roamed around the room.

"Don't you worry about it. I'm just glad you could make it." He smiled, his eyes crinkling at the corners. "Now tell me all about what my brilliant daughter has been up to."

Carmen laughed softly. "Oh, you know...nothing too exciting."

She proceeded to give vague updates about how fast Mia's learning and her new favorite foods and toys. All the while, her father listened intently, interjecting an occasional "That's because her mother is so attentive." or "That's my precious nieta."

Carmen soaked up his praise, pushing away the nagging guilt. She could pretend, just for one evening, that everything was fine.

All of a sudden, the cat knocked over a vase that was sitting on the console table up against the wall adjacent to where they were sitting. Alejandro called Lola to bring the broom and sweep the glass.

Carmen shifted uncomfortably on the sofa, her hands clasped tightly in her lap. She had hoped to keep the conversation light and breezy, but her father began asking probing questions and Lola's knowing glances were making it difficult to maintain her facade.

"So, how is the life of a pharmacy technician?" her father asked, leaning back in his leather chair.

"Well, you know...sick people, filling prescriptions. I've been working a lot of overtime lately," Carmen replied, trying to keep her tone casual.

Her father's brows furrowed. "Why so many hours lately? Is that knucklehead you're shacking up with not working again?"

Lola, who was still sweeping up broken glass from the cat's accident, gave a look that Carmen's father caught. He turned his attention back to Carmen, his eyes narrowing. "Spill it!"

Carmen nearly flatlined as she realized her secret was about to be exposed. "Well, me and..."

"When were you gonna tell us, Carmen?" her father interrupted.

Carmen's eyes bulged wide as her mother stepped out from the kitchen archway. "We know all about you living on your own," her mother confessed.

Carmen felt surprised, relieved, and a touch of anger all at the same time. She narrowed her eyes towards Lola and shifted her tightened lips to one side, silently questioning her cousin's loyalty.

Before anyone could say another word, the timer went off in the kitchen. "Dinner's ready!" her mother announced, breaking the tension in the room.

As they all moved towards the dining area, Carmen knew that the conversation was far from over. She would have to face the truth and deal with the consequences of her decisions, but for now, she was grateful for the temporary reprieve provided by her mother's call to dinner.

As they settled around the dinner table, Carmen's father, Alejandro, wasted no time in voicing his concerns about his daughter's living situation.

"I don't like it, Carmen. You're not safe. A woman shouldn't live alone, especially in a new county across town with no support system."

Carmen released air from her nostrils, pushing her food around on her plate. "I'm fine, Papá. I really am."

"Well, she has a friend that checks on her," Lola blurted out, immediately regretting her words as Carmen shot her a warning glance.

Carmen's mother perked up at this new information. "You have a new boyfriend?"

"Another loser?" Alejandro grumbled, his disapproval alive in his tone.

"No, he's an accountant," she responded, not appreciating her father's quick judgment of Jamal.

Her mother inquired. "Is he first or second generation citizen?"

As the cat snuggled underneath Alejandro's leg, Lola couldn't help but snicker. "His family has been here for a few hundred years."

Carmen's parents exchanged puzzled looks, clearly not understanding the implication of Lola's words. Carmen attempted to steer the conversation in a different direction, but her father persisted in discussing her new male friend.

Under the pressure of her father's insistence, Carmen accidentally let slip that Jamal was Black. The moment the words left her mouth, she knew she had made a mistake. The atmosphere in the room shifted dramatically as her parents' expressions changed from curiosity to clear disapproval.

Alejandro's face hardened, his jaw clenching as he processed this new information. Carmen's mother clasped her hands together, her forehead creased with concern. The silence that fell over the table was deafening, broken only by the soft purring of the cat beneath Alejandro's chair.

Alejandro's face contorted as he processed the information. "You're dating a Black guy?" he finally managed to speak after taking at least 3 minutes to get over the initial shock. "What the hell are you doing Carmen? You want to disgrace your father? What type of background is this joker from? Does he even know his father?"

The cat, picking up on the situation, quickly left its spot under the chair and ran off into a different room.

Carmen knew this conversation would be difficult, but she hadn't anticipated the level of hostility in her father's voice. "Yes, Papá. He grew up with both parents," Carmen defended, her voice trembling slightly but firm.

Her mother, who had been quiet all the while, finally spoke to gain clarity. "Shacking... co-parenting?"

"No, they were and still are very happily married."

Lola sat silently across the table, guilt across her face. She knew she had put Carmen in this awkward position by blabbing to her aunt and uncle. All she could do now was stuff her face, not wanting to get on her uncle's bad side, especially since she lived there.

The tension in the room was unmistakable as Alejandro's face reddened, his anger visibly growing. Carmen's mother looked torn between her husband's rage and her daughter's defiance. The meant to be pleasant family dinner had devolved into a battleground of cultural expectations and generational differences.

•••••●•●•••••

That night, Tony came over to visit Mia. Carmen watched as he played with their daughter, his face lighting up with genuine affection. For a brief moment, she caught a glimpse of the man she had once fallen for, the one who could be charming and attentive when he wanted to be.

After Mia fell asleep, Tony settled onto the couch next to Carmen. He cleared his throat, appearing almost remorseful.

"Last week, you said you needed money for your car payment. Well, I helped my homeboy paint a few houses, and I can break you off about $500."

Carmen's eyebrows shot up in surprise. "Really? That's nice of you."

For a moment, she thought about the child support paperwork she had filed earlier that day, wondering if she had been too hasty in her decision. Tony seemed to be making an effort, after all.

But as Tony scooted closer, his hand finding its way between her thighs, Carmen realized the money came with the usual strings attached. His fingers traced lazy circles on her lady parts, and she felt a usual mix of desire and resignation.

"Come on, Car," he murmured, his breath hot against her ear. "It's been a while."

Despite her better judgment, Carmen gave in to Tony's advances. Their bodies moved together with the familiarity of long-time lovers, but something felt off. As they finished, Carmen was left with a hollow feeling in the pit of her stomach.

While Tony was in the bathroom, his phone buzzed on the coffee table. Carmen glanced over, catching sight of a text message from somebody named Dreka. The preview showed just enough for Carmen to see the words "*miss you*" and a string of heart emojis.

Realization dawned on her. Dreka was the name of a tramp who lived in Tony's apartment complex. The guilt Carmen had felt earlier evaporated, replaced by anger and relief. She had made the right decision in filing for child support after all.

Carmen's voice trembled with anger and disbelief. "Dreka? You're screwing that hoe and me too? How long has this been going on Tony?"

Tony's face contorted. He scrambled for an excuse, his mind racing to find a plausible explanation. "She's been needing a ride lately due to car troubles," he lied, the words tumbling out unconvincingly.

Carmen's eyes narrowed, seeing through his flimsy excuse. "What are you mad for? If I was fucking her, you left me, remember?" Tony shot back, desperate for an out.

"Get out Tony," Carmen spat, her voice cold and final.

Tony dressed quickly, avoiding Carmen's piercing gaze. As he made his way to the door, Carmen threw on her robe and followed him, ready to lock up behind him.

Before shutting the door, Carmen held out her hand. "You forgot to give me the money," she reminded.

Tony stared at her for a moment, words seemingly on the tip of his tongue. Instead, he reached into his pants pocket, pulled out his wallet, and counted out $500 into her outstretched hand.

Their eyes locked for a brief moment, a silent exchange of unspoken words and emotions. Carmen looked away first, overcome with shame as she closed the door.

Alone in her apartment, the reality of what had just transpired hit her like a lightening bolt. "What have I turned into? I can't keep doing this. I can't keep doing this," she cried, tears releasing from her eyes, pooling down her face like a sudden flood. The room seemed to close in around her as Carmen slid down against the door, her body wracked with sobs. The $500 in her hand felt like a burning reminder of her compromised values, of the desperation that had led her to this point. She had never felt so cheap and worthless.

Chapter 15

Jamal's House

Jamal Adams

Jamal glanced around his kitchen, double-checking that he had all the ingredients handy to get dinner started. He wasn't a chef, but he was excellent at following instructions. Jamal flipped on his laptop that sat on the kitchen counter.

As it booted up he imagined Carmen's pretty smile-those white teeth and the twinkle in her eyes when she looked at him. "Here we go," he said as the screen requested his password. He went to YouTube, then to a popular chef's page that he followed.

From there, he found the video he was looking for-fall off the bone barbecue lamb chops, brown rice and spinach. The spinach wasn't just ordinary spinach. The chef added extra pow to it to give it more flavor. Jamal made sure that he followed the chef's recipe to the tee, leaving no room for error. He placed his garlic, rosemary and onion spices back on the spice rack when he was done.

"Perfect timing, he said looking at the clock on the kitchen wall. She should be here in a few minutes." He quickly threw the outfit on that he'd ironed earlier and spritzed on a little cologne-One Million by Paco Rananne Versace.

Within minutes, Carmen knocked on the door. Jamal was in awe when he opened it. She stood before him, a vision of beauty that surpassed even his most vivid imagination.

She had been always hot, but it was like she'd spent extra effort on herself this time. Her eyes, accentuated with smoky shadow and mascara, lips painted a deep, alluring red, curved into a smile that made Jamal weak at the knees. Her spring sundress, with its light fabric, swayed gently against her skin in the evening breeze.

"Wow... just wow!" Jamal breathed, unable to contain his awe.

Carmen's efforts hadn't gone unnoticed. She'd spent hours preparing, hot curling each strand of her hair to perfection. Jamal could feel his manhood knocking at the door of his pants to get out and introduce himself to the lovely Senorita Diaz.

"Come in, please. Dinner is actually ready," he grinned, closing the door and taking gentle hold of her fingertips. They were moist with nervous energy, a detail that didn't escape Jamal's notice, though he kept his expression neutral.

As he led her into the dining room, Carmen's eyes roamed over the interior of his home. The tasteful decor and spacious layout impressed her.

"You have a really nice home for a bachelor," she remarked. "Looks more like something for a married couple with kids."

The dining room was a picture of romantic ambiance. A fancy tablecloth laced the table, punctuated by sparkling candles. The dimmer switch was set low, giving a warm, intimate glow to the room.

Jamal pulled out a chair for Carmen. "Thank you. I figured that I made enough to go ahead and purchase a forever home. So, why not?" He shrugged. "This way, when I do get married and start a family, we won't have to move. Four bedrooms and 3.5 baths, should be enough to hold us for a good decade or more."

Jamal had actually purchased the home a few months before Kelis decided to become a traveling nurse and left Georgia. He'd planned on proposing but missed the opportunity. He didn't want to share this with Carmen though, not right now at least.

Jamal retreated back into the kitchen to grab the food. It made sense, what he'd said. Jamal was such a planner. He had it all together. He and Tony were like night and day. But, Carmen felt guilty comparing Mia's father to another man. She felt even more guilty wishing that Mia could be raised by her and Jamal instead of her and Tony.

Tony wanted them to be a family still. And maybe that might be how it should have, could have been, but...After the other night, seeing Dreka's name in his phone...there was no way she could entertain the thought of being with Tony again. He was irresponsible. Selfish. Manipulative. Untrustworthy. Lazy.

Carmen's eyes lit up as Jamal placed the dishes of food on the table. "This looks amazing," she said, clearly impressed by his culinary skills. "Are those lamb chops?"

Carmen blushed a little, realizing she had never actually tried them before. "Yes, they are. Do you like them?" Jamal asked.

"Never tried them, actually," Carmen admitted, feeling a bit embarrassed by her lack of exposure to finer cuisine.

"Well, I'm glad your first time will be with me," he responded with a smile as he went back into the kitchen.

He returned with a bottle of wine and proceeded to pour them each a glass.

Finally taking his seat next to Carmen, they began to chat animatedly as they ate. Jamal complimented her on how gorgeous she looked, from her hair to her mini sundress. Carmen returned the praise, telling him what an amazing cook he was.

"I've never had a guy cook anything for me that wasn't boiled or popped in the microwave," she remarked.

"Really? That's shocking," Jamal said, clearly surprised, losing himself in her eyes. The undeniable chemistry between them was inescapable now. In fact, Carmen was finding it harder and harder by the minute to breathe normally.

"Why is that so hard to believe?" she asked coyly.

"You're so sweet and beautiful. What man wouldn't live to make you happy?"

Carmen blushed fiercely, closing her eyes for a moment. No man had ever appreciated her the way Jamal did. But, she really hadn't experienced many, just Tony and her high-school sweetheart.

The playlist Jamal had playing quietly in the background, continued setting the mood as they chewed the last of what was on their plates and finished up their wine. Like always, sitting so close to Jamal, Carmen could feel her lady parts dampening. He smelled so damn good. Every whiff of him elevated her arousal level more.

"Carmen..." he stalled a moment peering straight through her soul. " I don't want to be your friend anymore."

She felt her whole-body collapse from a heart attack, but she was still sitting there. What was he saying? Why was this happening? Why did he invite her to his home, cook a romantic candlelight dinner just to...break her heart?

"Wha-t...what are you saying?" she managed to stammer, barely loud enough to be heard.

Jamal leaned in closer, his gaze never wavering. "Carmen...I want to be your man. I have feelings for you that I can't ignore. I want you to be my girlfriend. Or, we can't keep doing this, seeing each other."

Carmen's eyes threatened to drift away, but she forced herself to hold his gaze, albeit weakly. She swallowed hard, her throat constricting around the lump that had formed there. Her mind struggled, weighing her deep-seated trust issues and her parents' disapproval against the undeniable connection she felt with Jamal.

After what felt like an eternity, Carmen made her decision. "I want to be with you too," she replied, her voice soft but sure.

Jamal stroked her cheek gently. He kissed her lips, exploring their texture. Her mouth opened slightly, inviting his tongue to dance with hers. He slid the straps of her sundress down her arms, exposing her nipples.

As the kiss deepened, he teased her spine with his fingertips, pulling her bare chest closer. He swooped her up and carried her to the master bedroom, laying her gently on the bed, pulling her buttocks to the edge.

He finished undressing her, removing her panties. She raised up to see. "Lay back down and relax," he instructed with heated eyes. Carmen did as she was instructed, looking forward to what he would do next.

He suckled her nipples, then moved his mouth downward, teasing her skin with soft butterfly kisses. He continued his descent until he reached her honeypot. His tongue lapped at her honey, savoring it like a long-awaited treat.

Carmen arched her back, her moans filling the room as Jamal's tongue worked its magic. He knew just how to touch her, how to make her body sing. He explored her folds, his tongue darting and swirling, bringing her closer and closer to the edge.

“Jamal,” she gasped, her fingers gripping his hair. “Oh, Jamal...”

He continued his ministrations, the intensity building and Carmen's moans grew louder, her body writhing beneath him. Carmen had never experienced anything like this. She moaned, grabbing his head, rolling her hips to the motion of his mouth. Lost in the sensation, she couldn't comprehend what he was doing, only that he was a pleasure expert, deserving of recognition. "And the best 'Head Award' goes to Jamal Adams," she announced in her head, as fireworks sparked and toes curled.

Chapter 16

Unimpressed

Carmen Diaz

The air conditioning didn't seem to be giving much relief as the outdoor temperature soared to a sweltering 97 degrees. Carmen finished packing Mia's overnight bag, preparing her for a weekend stay at Auntie Felicia's house. Felicia didn't mind at all; in fact, she loved having Mia over. Despite not having children of her own, Felicia adored kids. Her focus was her career as an event planner – her true passion and talent. She ate, slept, and breathed event planning, content without a husband or kids for the time being. Besides, she was gorgeous, intelligent and only twenty-six, she would still be able to pull a husband in a few years when she was ready.

"Rabbit!" Mia fussed, reminding Carmen of her favorite stuffed animal.

"Oh baby, I'm sorry. I almost forgot your rabbit. Do you want to take the big one Jamal bought you too?" Mia's eyes lit up at the idea of bringing the gigantic plush rabbit Jamal had gifted her. She had been inseparable from the oversized toy since receiving it.

The doorbell rang as Carmen emerged from Mia's room, carrying the giant rabbit. "Hey babe," she greeted Jamal with a kiss on the lips. He had arrived, eager to depart and avoid being late for dinner - the first time he would meet Carmen's parents. He loaded up the Infinity with Mia's things that were gathered near the front door, while Carmen collected her daughter and the two rabbits. She knew Mia would want to sit on the backseat next to them as they headed to drop her off at Felicia's.

• • • • • • • • • • • •

As Jamal headed to Rex, his grip around the steering wheel got tighter. Despite the AC, the air in the car felt dense with unspoken apprehension.

"So, uh, what should I expect tonight?" Jamal finally asked.

Carmen's gaze shifted from the window to his face. She could see the worry in his furrowed brow. "They 're... traditional. But once they see how good you are for me, I'm sure they'll come around."

Jamal's eyes flipped to the rearview mirror, catching a glimpse of Mia hugging her oversized rabbit. "And they know about...?"

"Yeah, they do." Carmen's voice dropped . "Look, I won't lie. They're not thrilled about the whole interracial thing. But you're a good man, Jamal. You're stable, hardworking. You treat Mia like she's your own."

The car slowed at a red light, and Jamal turned to face Carmen. "I just don't want to make things harder for you, Car. If they can't accept me — "

"Then that's their problem," Carmen cut in. "You've been nothing but amazing to us. They need to see that."

From the backseat, Mia's voice piped up, "Mal good!"

A smile creased on Jamal's lips, some of the worry easing. "Thanks, princess."

As they pulled up to Felicia's house, Carmen reached over and squeezed Jamal's hand. "Just be yourself tonight. That's more than enough."

Jamal nodded, but the worry hadn't completely left his eyes. "And if it's not?"

"Then we'll figure it out together. You're part of our lives now, Jamal. I'm not letting anyone change that."

Carmen gently kissed Jamal's cheek before gathering Mia and her belongings. As they approached

Felicia's front door, the summer heat clung to their skin. Felicia greeted them with a peppy smile, her eyes stretched as they landed on Jamal.

"You said he was good looking... I didn't realize how much. The pictures you've shown of him didn't do him justice." She playfully fanned her face with her hand.

"Now, watch it now," Carmen said, with a jokey hint of possessiveness.

Jamal's cheeks warmed at the compliment. "Thanks, nice meeting you."

As Felicia placed Mia onto her hip, Jamal brought in the rabbits. Mia's laughter bubbled up at the sight of them. With her free hand, Felicia made a subtle 'call me later' gesture to Carmen before closing the door.

Back in the car, Jamal inhaled deeply and let out a heavy breath. Carmen reached over, her fingers intertwining with his. "It's going to be fine," she reassured him. She turned the radio to a more upbeat station. As Carmen began to sing along, her voice slightly off-key, Jamal's tension visibly eased.

He chuckled. "You are beautiful, but... not the best singer I see."

Carmen playfully swatted his shoulder, her laughter joining his. "Turn into this subdivision," she directed, "they'll be the last house on the left."

As Jamal guided the car into the driveway, the engine's purr faded to silence. Inside the house, Carmen's father's keen ears picked up the sound. He peered out the living room window. "They're here," he announced to Maria.

Maria moved towards the front door. She put on a smile, but it lacked sincerity as she braced herself to greet Carmen and Jamal.

As Carmen and Jamal settled onto the sofa in the living room, Alejandro's scrutinizing gaze bore into them. He wasted no time to begin his interrogation.

"So, Jamal," Alejandro began, "tell me about your upbringing."

Jamal straightened his posture, meeting Alejandro's eyes. "I was raised in Atlanta, sir. My parents instilled strong values in me. Hard work, respect, and family."

"And your career? What do you do?"

"I'm an accountant at J.S. Barnes & Associates. I've been there for five years now."

"Salary?"

Carmen winced at her father's bluntness, but Jamal remained composed. "I make $83,000 annually, sir."

A fleeting expression, maybe reluctant acceptance, appeared on Alejandro's face before disappearing. Carmen sensed an opening and jumped in.

"Papá, Jamal is wonderful with Mia. He's so patient and caring—"

Alejandro cut her off with a wave of his hand. "That's good, but a man needs to provide more than just affection."

"He does," Carmen insisted. "He reminds me a lot of you, Papá. Dependable, hardworking-"

Alejandro's jaw tightened, clearly uncomfortable with the comparison. Jamal shifted on the cushion, feeling Alejandro's disapproval.

The room was becoming suffocating when Lola's voice rang out from the kitchen, "Dinner's ready!"

Carmen and Jamal stood up quickly, eager to escape the oppressive vibes. The aroma of tinga (a savory blend of chicken, tomatoes, and smoky chipotle) swept from the dining room, a momentary time out from the uncomfortable interrogation. As they followed Alejandro to the table, Carmen squeezed Jamal's hand, a silent apology and reassurance. Jamal returned the gesture. They knew the battle was far from over.

As they ate, Jamal complimented Carmen's mom Maria, and her cousin Lola's culinary skills. Lola smiled and opened up to friendly conversation, letting Jamal know that Carmen is always bragging to her about how great he is.

"She's always going on about how amazing you are with Mia and what a great chef you are."

Jamal ducked his head, a bashful grin on his face. "Well, Mia's an easy kid to love. And Carmen... she's pretty special too. I'm okay in the kitchen, I guess."

Alejandro looked unimpressed and Maria uncomfortable, changed the subject as Jamal and Lola engaged in friendly banter. She decided to ask Jamal about his parents and if he had any siblings.

Jamal answered, speaking all positive experiences and achievements when it came to his family, including the fact that his sister is an A student at college.

"What school, and what's her major?" Lola asked, genuinely interested.

"Georgia State University, Computer Science," Jamal replied with pride evident in his voice.

Alejandro chimed in the conversation, and his voice became noticeably harsh. "Here's the thing Jamal, the thing no one wants to say - you're a Black guy. Being Black is not a great thing in America or anywhere else. No matter how great you do, people will always see it as nothing. Do you want that for Carmen? I want my daughter to have the best."

The table went silent for a moment, as everyone absorbed Alejandro's words. Jamal's jaw tightened, his eyes narrowing as he processed the blatant racism.

"So, are you saying that it's better for her to be with a Hispanic American or a White American or any other American who may not even have a job, a house or treat her with respect, just as long as he's not me?" Jamal's voice reached a crescendo, his anger and hurt obvious to everyone sitting there.

"First off, you will lower your voice in this house!" Alejandro demanded, his own voice rising to match Jamal's. "And it's not just you! That's *any* Black man that threatens to impregnate my daughter with negro kids."

Everyone's eyes bucked out of disbelief at Alejandro's callous words. Maria gasped, her hand flying to her mouth. Lola stared at her uncle in shock, her mouth agape. Carmen's face flushed with anger and embarrassment.

Jamal felt completely dehumanized in that moment. He stood abruptly, his chair scraping against the floor. "Carmen, let's go," he said, his eyes never leaving Alejandro's.

Carmen paused, torn between her love for Jamal and the deeply ingrained respect for her father. "I'll be out in a minute," she spoke low, her eyes pleading with Jamal to understand.

Jamal sat in the car, gripping the steering wheel tightly. Anger radiated from him like heat from a furnace.

"What the hell could she possibly have to say to them? Fuck!" He slammed his fist on the dashboard, his frustration echoing in the confines of the vehicle.

Every passing moment felt like a punch to his gut. He couldn't lose Carmen over this. But how could he endure being with her while facing her parents' bigotry?

The front door swung open, and Carmen emerged angry and distressed. Jamal looked over at her father, who was standing at the doorway, angrily wagging his finger. Jamal strained to catch their conversation but only caught snippets.

"You best make the right choice!"

She quickly got in the passenger's seat of Jamal's car, to escape his tirade.

"What the hell is that man saying now?" Jamal questioned as he stormed out of the driveway, nearly clipping the mailbox with his car.

"Calm down, Jamal! You're speeding!" Carmen said, her voice quaking with fear as she clutched her seatbelt.

"Just answer my fuckin' question!" He snapped, anger coursing through him like wildfire.

Carmen blinked, surprised by his tone. This wasn't like him at all.

"Stop cursing at me," she replied firmly.

Jamal was hit with a sudden realization of his tone; he softened immediately. "I'm sorry. I didn't mean... I just don't understand what more you have to say to them."

Carmen's eyes fell momentarily. "He's my father. They're my parents. I was just trying—"

"Trying to make sure you were still good with them? After they completely disrespected me?"

"It's not like that, Jamal! They're stuck in their ways..."

Jamal let out an incredulous laugh as he pressed harder on the gas pedal, merging onto the highway toward Newnan. "Maybe we should've just picked up Mia," he muttered under his breath.

"I thought I was staying at your house this weekend?" Carmen asked tentatively, shifting in her seat.

"Maybe we should turn around."

"Jamal?"

"I thought a lot of things too, Car." He gritted his teeth, furious. "I thought that if some shit like this went down, I could count on you to fight with me and not straddle the fuckin' fence."

Chapter 17

Booty Call

Carmen Diaz

"I *thought a lot of things too, Car.*" He gritted his teeth, furious. "I *thought that if some shit like this went down, I could count on you to fight with me and not straddle the fuckin' fence.*" That's what Jamal had said in the car two days ago, after the disastrous dinner at Carmen's parents' home. Before he changed their plans and took her to her house instead of his.

Carmen pulled another prescription bottle from the shelf, scanning the label twice before dumping tablets into the counting tray. She could feel a dull ache behind her eyes. Three customers deep in line, and the woman at the counter kept tapping her credit card against the counter like a metronome.

"Ma'am, your insurance requires prior authorization for—"

"I've been taking this medication for six months."

Carmen's jaw locked. "The policy changed. We can call your doctor, but it'll take a few days."

The woman's nostrils flared. "This is ridiculous. I need it today."

Behind her, someone sighed loud enough to carry. Another muttered something about incompetence.

Mr. Hancock materialized at Carmen's shoulder, his cologne potent enough to choke on. "Pick up the pace, Diaz." His breath tickled her ear. "Remember, I'm watching. You've been doing better, but that doesn't mean you can slack off now."

She nodded, swallowing the words she wanted to spit back. Her phone vibrated in her pocket—once, twice. She ignored it, processing the next customer, then the next, her smile stretching as thin as plastic wrap.

Break couldn't come fast enough.

Carmen ducked into the back room, pulling her phone out before the door even clicked shut. Jamal's name lit up the screen. Her heart kicked.

He hadn't answered her calls. Hadn't responded to her texts for two days straight.

She opened the messages.

"I was just returning your call."

She typed to reply back, typing, erasing, then starting over...

"*I'm so sorry about my dad. He was completely out of line. You know I'm on your side, right? Always. Please don't doubt that.*"

The typing bubble appeared. Disappeared. Appeared again.

"*I know. I forgive you.*"

Relief flooded through her chest.

"*Can you come over tonight? After Mia's asleep?*"

"*Booty call?*"

Carmen snorted despite herself.

"*More like makeup sex.*"

A pause.

"*Why not have dinner and all that, instead of just 'makeup sex'?*"

She glanced at the clock on the wall.

"*I'm helping Felicia paint her home office and do some redecorating. So I'm eating with her likely.*"

Another pause. Then:

"*Alright. I'll come by later.*"

Carmen exhaled, shoulders dropping. The knot in her stomach loosened, just a fraction. Two days of silence, of replaying that dinner in her head, her father's sneer, Jamal's expression, the way she should have shut it all down completely.

"*Thank you,*" she typed.

Mr. Hancock's voice carried through the door. "Diaz! Break's over!"

She shoved the phone back in her pocket and pushed through the door, the weight in her chest a little lighter than it had been fifteen minutes ago.

•••••••••••

Carmen pressed her lips to Mia's forehead, lingering just long enough to feel the warmth of her daughter's sleep-steady breath. Her tiny fingers were curled around the edge of her blanket. Carmen tucked it tighter around her before easing the door shut and returning her own room.

Carmen's room smelled of the vanilla body spray she'd just spritzed over her collarbones. The black lace bralette barely covered anything, the matching panties riding high on her hips. The silk of her robe slipped open as she leaned into the mirror to swipe gloss across her lips. The wine she'd poured earlier sat half-empty on the nightstand.

A knock at the door—two firm raps, then a pause. Jamal's signature.

She opened it, and there he stood in gray sweatpants, the outline of his bulge unmistakable beneath the fabric. His graphic tee stretched across his chest, the sleeves tight around his biceps. His gaze dragged down her body, slow, hungry.

"Damn," he murmured, stepping inside.

Carmen smirked, taking his hand and pulling him in. "You like?"

His thumb brushed the lace at her hip. "You know I do."

She poured him a glass, the wine glinting burgundy as it filled. Then she led him to her bedroom where they sat on her bed. They clinked glasses, the quiet between them comfortable as their chemistry became even more charged.

"Your dad still pissed you're with me?" Jamal took a sip, watching her over the rim.

Carmen rolled her eyes. "He'll get over it." She said this but didn't believe it.

"Or he won't."

"Then that's his problem." She set her glass down, moving closer to him. "I don't care what he thinks."

Jamal's fingers traced the curve of her waist, slipping beneath the robe. "You sure about that?"

She kissed him instead of answering, her mouth hot and insistent. His hands tightened, pulling her body against him. The robe hit the floor first. Then his shirt. His sweatpants followed, pooling around his ankles. The bed creaked as he laid her back, his lips trailing down her neck, lower, lower.

Carmen arched, her fingers twisting in the sheets. "Jamal—"

He didn't make her wait before giving her what she really craved, which was him inside her.

The headboard knocked against the wall, stroking steady, relentless. Her breath came in sharp gasps, his name a broken chant between her lips. His hands gripped her hips, holding her exactly where he wanted her.

Carmen arched her back, pressing her palms flat against the mattress as she raised her legs higher, hooking them over Jamal's shoulders. His grip tightened on her hips, fingers digging into the soft flesh as he drove deeper, each thrust more intense. She gasped, her nails scraping the sheets, the friction between them unbearable.

"Fuck—" The word tore from her throat, ragged.

Jamal growled low in his chest, his strokes relentless. The heat coiled tighter in her belly, her muscles clenching around him. She could feel the sweat slick between their bodies, the way his breath hitched when she rocked back against him, meeting every stroke.

Then his hands slid to her waist, gripping it, lifting her as they came off the bed. He prompted her to place her feet on the floor as he put her down. "Turn over."

She didn't hesitate. Carmen turned away from Jamal and bent over, bracing herself at the edge of the bed, her feet planted firm on the floor. The shift made her feel exposed, vulnerable, completely at his mercy. But she loved it!

Jamal didn't waste time. His hands smoothed up her thighs, spreading her wider before he gripped her hips again, pulling her back against him. The first thrust was brutal, deep, stealing her breath. She cried out, her fingers twisting in the sheets, her back bowing under the force of it.

"Like that?" He asked, knowing she loved every inch of him.

"Yes—" The word dissolved into a moan as he set a merciless pace, each snap of his hips sending shockwaves through her. The bedframe groaned beneath them, the headboard thudding against the wall in time with their ragged breathing.

Carmen bending completely over now, pressed her forehead into the mattress, her body trembling, every nerve alight. She could feel him everywhere—the heat of his skin against hers, the grip of his fingers, the relentless drag of his big hard flesh inside her.

Jamal leaned over her, his chest pressed against her back, his mouth hot at her ear. "You take me so fucking good."

She shuddered, her thighs shaking. The pleasure built, sharp and unrelenting, tightening low in her stomach. She was close, so close...

His hand slid around her hip, fingers finding her clit, circling just right.

Carmen shattered.

Her vision whited out, her body locking around him as the orgasm ripped through her, violent, consuming. Jamal cursed, his rhythm faltering, then he buried himself deep one last time, his groan muffled against her shoulder as he came.

For a long moment, neither of them moved. Their breaths mingled, heavy, uneven. Then Jamal pressed a kiss to the damp skin between her shoulder blades before easing away.

Carmen collapsed onto the bed, her limbs liquid, her pulse still thundering in her ears. Jamal stretched out beside her, his fingers tracing idle patterns along her spine.

She turned her head, meeting his gaze. His dark eyes were hooded, satisfied.

Carmen smirked. "So..."

Jamal raised an eyebrow. "So?"

She reached for her wineglass, taking a slow sip. "Still worried about my dad?"

He laughed, low and rich, pulling her against him. "Nah." His thumb brushed her bottom lip. "You're definitely worth it." They both laughed lazily as she sat the wine glass back down.

For a long moment, the only sound was their breathing. Then Jamal chuckled, rolling onto his back. "Guess we made up."

Carmen swatted his chest, laughing. "Shut up."

He pulled her against him, her head finding its place on his shoulder. The wine sat forgotten, the night stretching quiet around them.

Chapter 18

Leaps of Faith

Carmen Diaz

Risk-taking had never been Carmen's forte, but lately, she found herself taking leaps of faith more often than not. From moving out of the house with Tony to avoiding calls from her mother for the past few weeks, she was stepping out of her comfort zone. She didn't even want to think about her father and the disastrous dinner they'd had. She and Jamal tried their best not to mention anything related to him. These days, all they focused on was each other. Things seemed to be getting better. She'd even gotten an update regarding the child support petition. Tony had been served.

She assumed that's why he'd been blowing up her phone like crazy on a Saturday morning.

"Car, your phone," Jamal said groggily, laying next to her.

"It's nothing. Probably Felicia texting me, excited about the date she went on last night. Go back to sleep."

Felicia hadn't texted. It was all Tony. But, Carmen definitely didn't want Jamal getting worked up about it. She'd almost lost him because of her parents' prejudiced views. There was no way she was going to let Tony get between them. Carmen grabbed the phone off her nightstand and cut the power off. She then rolled over and forced herself back to sleep for about two more hours, since it was only 4:24 am according to her phone screen .

When Carmen woke back up, she heard Jamal humming in the bathroom. The melody was familiar. It was 'Wait for Love' by Luther Vandross, the song they had made love to last night. A closed-lip grin spread wide across her face as she reminisced.

She decided to get started on breakfast before Mia woke up in the room next door. Slipping out of bed quietly, Carmen headed to the tiny kitchen. As she cracked eggs into a bowl, she heard the bathroom door open.

"Mmm, something smells good in here," Jamal said, emerging freshly showered and dressed in a graphic tee and khaki cargo shorts. He grabbed plates and glasses from the cupboard to help set the table.

"How'd you sleep?" Carmen asked, whisking the eggs.

"I should be asking you that," he chuckled. "With all the notifications blowing up your phone last night, seems like you got some guys lining up."

Carmen laughed. "Trust me, none of the guys I know can even compete with you."

She hoped he would drop the subject of her phone. She didn't want to ruin their weekend by talking about Tony. Luckily, the pitter patter of tiny feet running into the kitchen provided a distraction.

Mia hugged Carmen's leg tightly. "Mama!" Then she spotted Jamal and giggled. "Mal!" she exclaimed, surprised to see him so early. She had been asleep when he came over last night. Jamal had been dropping by a lot more frequently after that night he and Carmen made up.

Carmen scooped the eggs onto plates beside bacon and biscuits. She grabbed the orange juice from the fridge for Jamal to pour. A family breakfast together was just the distraction she needed.

Carmen, Jamal, and Mia sat around the small kitchen table, enjoying their breakfast together. Mia giggled as she smeared jam on her biscuit, while Carmen and Jamal exchanged naughty glances, reminiscing of last night.

"Anything in particular you want to do today?" Jamal asked, bringing a slice of bacon to his mouth.

"What's going on in Newnan today?" Carmen asked, sipping her coffee.

Jamal thought for a moment before listing off a few activities. "Well, there's a farmers market downtown, a new exhibit at the art gallery, a puppet show at the library, a nature walk at the park, and I think there's even a small carnival setting up on the outskirts of town."

Carmen's eyes lit up at the mention of the carnival. She knew Mia would love the bright colors and festive atmosphere. "What do you think, Mia? Want to go see the carnival?"

"Carnival! Carnival!"

Jamal chuckled. "Looks like we have a winner."

Just as Carmen was about to respond, the doorbell rang, interrupting their conversation. She glanced at the clock, surprised anyone would come at this early hour. "You expecting someone?" Jamal asked, concerned about her opening the door.

"No, but I did order some board books for Mia. Maybe they arrived early."

Jamal stood up from the table. "Let me get it, just in case. And remind me to have a camera installed for you. That way, you can monitor visitors on your cell phone."

As Jamal made his way to the door, Carmen felt a sense of unease. She couldn't quite put her finger on it, but something felt off. When Jamal opened the door, she realized why. It wasn't a delivery worker. There, standing on the other side, was Tony-Antonio Lopez.

Tony gave a mean mug as he took in Jamal's presence. "What the fuck are you doing here this early in the morning?"

"Who the hell do you think you're talking to?"

"Talking to you, chump!" Tony spat.

"Chump?" Jamal repeated, amplifying his voice.

Carmen quickly intervened, not wanting the situation to escalate further. She could see Mia getting anxious, whimpering in her chair. "Hey, let's all calm down.

"My baby is getting upset." Tony pushed past Jamal and made his way into the kitchen. He picked Mia up from her chair, ignoring the biscuit clutched in her tiny hand. He pressed a kiss to her rosy cheek, his anger momentarily forgotten.

Jamal watched the interaction, his eyes never leaving Tony. "Again, why are you here, man?"

"You're asking me? I have a child here. I'm Mia's father, or have you forgotten?"

"Unfortunately, I can't forget that," Jamal muttered under his breath.

Carmen stepped between them, holding her hands up . "Hey, look, guys, let me put Mia in her playpen in her room, and then we can talk. She's about done with that biscuit."

Carmen slipped away to the back , leaving Tony and Jamal in a tense standoff. She quickly set up Mia's playpen, arranging her favorite toys and turning on the small television to distract her. When she returned, she took Mia from Tony's arms, and carried her to her room.

Carmen walked back to the front, giving Tony a stern look. "So, why are you here?" she asked, her arms folded across her chest.

Jamal watched the exchange, waiting for Tony's response.

Tony pulled a crumpled paper from his pocket, holding it up for Carmen to see. "This shit right here. They served me a few days ago-child support. Why Carmen? I'm doing my best helping out. Why you wanna screw me like that? Is it cause you think I'm smashing that bitch in my complex?"

"What?" Jamal reacted, puzzled at how Carmen would know who Tony was sleeping with and why she'd care."

Carmen shook her head. "I couldn't care less who you're sleeping with Tony. I'm with Jamal now. You and I are over." She spoke in code, hoping that Tony wouldn't reveal that not too long ago she and him were still screwing while she was asking Jamal to give her time to heal.

Jamal split his gaze between both Carmen and Tony.

"So, that explains why he's here early. You finally tested the forbidden fruit," Tony expelled a sarcastic chuckle.

Jamal gave Tony a warning stare.

Tony met Jamal's gaze with an evil eye. "Are you the one who had her to put me in the system?"

"No, he wasn't," Carmen responded quickly, before Jamal could.

" Carmen, please...rethink this. We got history. You know my situation. It's hard for me in the workforce. I'm trying. I want to make us work. For you, and for Mia especially. I do love both of you," Tony pleaded.

Jamal quickly shifted his eyes to Carmen to examine her response. She seemed affected by Tony's words, but why was unclear to Jamal. Did she feel he was being manipulative as always and was annoyed, or was she actually feeling something else... Was she considering starting over with him?

"Tony...I'm doing what I feel is best for Mia. I'm sorry if that affects you negatively, but...she comes first."

"So, if she comes first, why are you leaving me, her father for this dude over here?" He pointed between himself and Jamal. "Let me tell our daughter bye before I go." Tony went to tell Mia goodbye. Then he left, not looking or speaking to Jamal or Carmen as he walked out the door, slamming it behind.

"Seems like we need to talk," Jamal stated. "Is there something I'm not aware of about you and Tony?"

"No, definitely not." Carmen attempted to reassure Jamal but he couldn't help but feel as if she was hiding something.

She could feel the heat of Jamal's eyes on her, sense his unease. Turning to face him, she knew she had to give him an explanation, without spilling all the facts.

"Jamal, I'm sorry you had to see all that. Tony showing up like this, it brings up a lot of old history and drama that I've been trying to move past."

She took Jamal's hand, leading him over to the couch so they could sit. "You have to understand, Tony and I have a long, messy history. We were together for years before it all went south. Being with you though, has shown me what a real, healthy relationship can be like.

But Tony, he knows how to get in my head, play on my emotions."

Jamal listened intently, nodding for her to continue.

"I won't lie, some part of me will always care about him because he's Mia's father. But I don't have any interest in rekindling a romantic relationship with him. That ship has sailed away."

She squeezed Jamal's hand, looking into his eyes earnestly. "You're the one I want to be with. I know it hasn't been easy, especially with my family's issues about us dating. But I'm committed to making this - us - work."

Jamal let out a breath he didn't realize he'd been holding. Hearing Carmen confirm her feelings for him washed away the doubts that had crept in.

"I'm glad we cleared this up. I trust you, Carmen. I just get worried when Tony comes around, trying to manipulate you and Mia. He doesn't seem to respect boundaries."

"You're right, he doesn't. But I'm learning to set those boundaries more firmly. Having you by my side makes me stronger."

She leaned in and kissed Jamal softly. Pulling back, she smiled. "Now, what do you say we get back to our fun family day and head to that carnival?"

Jamal returned her smile, although his doubt only slightly diminished. "That sounds perfect."

Chapter 19

Undeterred

Jamal Adams

Brandi stepped into Jamal's office, barely tapping the cracked door before gliding inside. She sashayed across the floor, hips swaying. The tailored fabric of her dress clung to her pencil waist, while her *assets* seemed to defy gravity. She had become relentless in her pursuit, and today felt no different.

"Hey there, Jamal," she purred, leaning against his desk, overly confident. "I was hoping we could chat a bit."

Jamal lifted his eyes from his computer screen, his brow furrowing at the unexpected interruption. He leaned back in his chair, creating distance between them as Brandi's perfume circulated through the office.

"I was wondering if you would be interested in accompanying me to a banquet this weekend." I need an escort. It's last minute and I've got no one." She pouted her lips.

"Brandi, we've talked about this," he said, wishing she'd just go away. "Us going out wouldn't be appropriate."

Undeterred, Brandi sat on the edge of his desk, crossing her legs deliberately. The hem of her dress inched higher, revealing more of her smooth, toned thighs. She tilted her head, dark waves cascading over one shoulder.

"Oh, come on, Jamal. Don't act like you don't notice me," she teased, her fingers tracing patterns on the polished wood. "I've seen the way you look at me when you think no one's watching."

He couldn't deny Brandi's beauty, but she wasn't his type. "That's enough, Brandi," he said, his voice strained. "This conversation is over."

Brandi leaned in closer, her lips curving into a seductive smile. "It doesn't have to be, you know. We could take this somewhere even more... private, after work."

Her hand reached out, fingers grazing Jamal's arm. He flinched, pulling away as if burned. The touch sent a signal to his lower extremities.

"I mean it, Brandi. I'm honestly not feeling you."

For a moment, hurt appeared in Brandi's eyes, but she shook it off. She stood, smoothing her dress with nonchalance.

"You can't deny the chemistry between us forever, Jamal. I could tell I was getting to you a few minutes ago. I'm patient. I can wait."

A faint sigh escaped his lips. "Brandi, I'm seeing someone right now."

Her brows arched playfully. "Carmen? You mean the single mom? I heard you and Tavaris talk about her in the breakroom. I get it; she's got that nurturing vibe going for her." She shrugged, dismissing the notion with a wave of her hand. "But you know we have chemistry."

"Chemistry doesn't mean much if it's built on bad timing. Besides, we don't have much in common." He forced himself to maintain eye contact, even though Brandi was overwhelming him. Jamal retrieved his phone from his desk drawer with Carmen's face featured on his front screen.

Brandi's eyes fell to the photo. She tilted her head slightly, smirking out the corner of her mouth. "You're one of those passport bros? No wonder... You don't date women my hue, I guess?"

Jamal frowned at the assumption. "Is that what you get from one glimpse of the woman I'm currently involved with? From that, you dissect my entire relationship history?"

"You're saying I'm wrong?" Brandi countered, crossing her arms defiantly.

"Very. I don't select my women based off of ethnicity. And just for the record, she was born and raised here."

"Sorry," she replied sincerely.

Jamal nodded, accepting Brandi's apology. There was a brief pause before Brandi spoke again.

"So what do you find attractive?"

He hesitated, unsure if he wanted to navigate that minefield. If he described what he valued in a partner—intelligence, modesty, kindness, loyalty—she would likely take offense.

Before he could respond further, Tavaris entered the office with his signature jovial energy.

"Well look who it is!" Tavaris exclaimed as he took in Brandi's presence. He walked over and flashed his charming smile at her. "You gracing us with your beauty again? Always a pleasure."

Brandi turned to Tavaris and flashed him an alluring smile. The pressure shifted as she straightened up and directed all attention toward him. Jamal remained silent but felt a sense of relief as Tavaris effortlessly stole the spotlight from Brandi's advances.

Brandi left Jamal's office, urging him to reconsider the banquet invite before clicking the door behind her. Jamal couldn't help but feel relieved.

"Ma-an! Did you see that badonk?" Tavaris barked.

Jamal, responded unphased. "Yeah, I saw it."

"Negro, you can't tell me that a glance at that chick doesn't make you get a rise in your pants."

Jamal uncomfortably recalled the involuntary reaction he had experienced when Brandi was in his office. "I'm committed to Carmen. Not thinking about Brandi."

"Man, you're missing out. That woman is fine as hell, and she's got a body that won't quit."

Jamal rolled his eyes, trying to ignore the image of Brandi's curves that were now firmly planted in his mind. "I'm not interested in her like that," he insisted.

Tavaris shook his head in disappointment. "You know, sometimes I think you're too good for your own damn good. You're turning down the chance to be with someone like Brandi? You got to use common sense instead of playing by the rules all the damn time."

"What's that supposed to mean?"

"I'm just saying, Carmen's got a lot of baggage, man. Her racist parents, her narcissistic ex...it's a lot to deal with."

Jamal's blood heated recalling the numerous times he had had to deal with Tony's antics. "It's not easy, but I love her," he said simply.

"I know you do, man. But just think about it. Brandi's got her shit together. She's ambitious, she's successful, and she's got a body that won't quit. What more could you want?"

Jamal shook his head, a small smile playing at the corners of his mouth. "As if Brandi wouldn't come with drama. You can look at that and tell there's crazy all behind it."

Tavaris grinned. "Hey, the crazy women have the best sex. I know that from experience."

"I bet you do."

Tavaris suddenly grew serious. "Man, for real thou gh...how are you handling that ex of hers popping up all the damn time and her family? Is she still talking to her dad after he dissed you like that at dinner?"

Jamal inhaled deeply before answering. "She hasn't spoken to her parents since. As for the ex, I don't know how much more I can take from his ass. He's a real piece of work, and I'm just trying not to knock his ass out. I don't want to do that. I do, but I don't. He's Mia's dad."

"I feel you, man. But just remember, I've got your back, no matter what."

"Thanks, man. I appreciate it."

Tavaris had barely left Jamal's office when a soft knock echoed through the room. Jamal, still gathering his thoughts from the previous conversation, called out a welcoming, "Come in." The door opened to reveal a woman whose age had painted her hair in streaks of silver and white, yet she carried herself with a grace that defied time. Her name was Mrs. Humphrey, a recent arrival in the world of successful entrepreneurs with her bakery in Lithonia.

"Good afternoon, Mr. Adams," she greeted, her voice carrying a touch of the South. "I hope I'm not too early."

Jamal stood and extended his hand. "Right on time, Mrs. Humphrey. Please, have a seat."

As they sat, Mrs. Humphrey began to unfold the story of her bakery's recent success. The numbers, once manageable, had grown to a point where they were no longer just promising—they were overwhelming. She needed help, someone to navigate the financial seas that her business was now sailing.

Jamal listened attentively, nodding at all the right moments, his mind already working on solutions. He outlined his services, explaining his fees and the value he could bring to her growing business. Mrs. Humphrey seemed pleased with his proposals.

As the consultation came to a close, Jamal's phone buzzed on his desk. It was Carmen.

"Jamal, I'm in the area. I get an hour today because I'm working a ten-hour shift. Do you want to grab a quick bite?"

"Absolutely, Carmen. I'll meet you at the steak house nearby."

They said their goodbyes, and as he pocketed his phone, Jamal found himself lost in thought. Tavaris' words about Tony and Carmen's parents played through his mind. He thought about his own family, their expectations, and the potential disapproval they might harbor for the challenges he was facing with Carmen's ex and her family.

His father had warned about the complexities of interracial relationships, the cultural clashes, and the societal pressures that could ensue. Yet, despite all these potential pitfalls, Jamal had willingly walked into this relationship, his love for Carmen outweighing any obstacle in their path.

It was in this moment of reflection that Jamal truly acknowledged the depth of his feelings for Carmen. He loved her, deeply and without reserve. It was a truth he had known in his heart, but saying it out loud to Tavaris had somehow solidified it, made it real in a way that he could no longer ignore or downplay. Jamal shut down his laptop and locked up his office. He had a lunch date with the woman he loved, and he wasn't going to let anyone or anything distract him from that.

Chapter 20

Something Amiss

Jamal Adams

There was a large lunch crowd at the steak house as Jamal pulled into the parking lot. After circling around a few times, he found a spot and parked, then made his way inside to where Carmen was waiting. As soon as their eyes met, he could tell something was amiss. The usual sparkle in her deep brown eyes was dimmed, she seemed to have something troubling on her mind.

"Hey." Jamal slid into the booth across from her. "Everything okay?"

Carmen let out a heavy breath before answering. "I just got off the phone with Lola before you came. It seems my parents want to see Mia for her birthday."

"Is that what's bothering you?" He reached out and covered her hand with his .

"I don't know if taking Mia there is a good idea," Carmen admitted, biting her lip. "But I also don't want to keep them apart on her special day. I feel like it would be punishing Mia somehow."

"I think I might have a solution," Jamal said, squeezing her hand before pulling back, becoming more serious. "Why don't you have your parents come to your place? On your terms, of course. Then you'd be the one in control."

"I...I'm not sure I want them to see how small my house is," she confessed in a noticeably lower pitch. "How little I have compared to what they're used to seeing me with."

"Don't sell yourself short. You do an amazing job taking care of Mia on your own. Your home may be modest, but it's full of love. That's what truly matters." He paused, studying her expression carefully before asking his next question.

"Have you heard anything from Tony recently?" The mention of him had Carmen tensing up instantly.

"He texted me a few days ago..."

"And?"

"He wanted me to drop the child support petition and come back to him." A bitter laugh escaped her lips.

"As if I'd ever consider going back after everything he's done."

"You didn't respond though?"

"No. You were right last time. Ignoring him is for the best."

"I think it's important to set clear boundaries with Tony, even when it comes to visitation. Maybe suggest scheduled visits, so he can't just pop up whenever he feels like it," Jamal proposed.

"I know you're right, but I'm worried about how he'll react. He's never been good at following rules or respecting boundaries."

"We'll handle it together. And if he can't abide by the terms you set, then he'll have to face the consequences of going to court about that too."

The server approached their table. He was a somewhat dorky looking young guy with thick glasses and a friendly smile on his face. "Are you folks ready to order?"

Jamal glanced at the menu briefly before responding. "I'll have the ribeye, medium-rare, with a loaded baked potato and a side salad."

"And for you, ma'am?" The server turned to Carmen.

"The grilled chicken Caesar salad, please," she replied, handing over her menu.

As the server departed with their orders, Jamal turned his attention back to Carmen discussing their relationship challenges. "I know our families haven't been the most supportive of our relationship. But we can't let their disapproval dictate our lives."

"I just wish my parents could see past the color of your skin and recognize what an amazing man you are."

"And I wish my family could understand that the obstacles we face only make us stronger. But at the end of the day, it's our love that matters most. We'll get through all these challenges together, no matter what."

Carmen gazed across the table, her eyes locked with Jamal's. The reality of what he'd just said hit her like a hundred mile per hour brick. "Love?" she echoed, faintly.

Jamal's heart pounded in his chest. He hadn't planned on confessing his feelings so abruptly, but there it was, bare and vulnerable for her to see. "I love you, Carmen Diaz," he declared, the words flowing from a place of unguarded truth.

Carmen's eyes glistened with unshed tears, her breath hitching in her throat. The gravity of his admission struck a chord , resonating with her own unspoken feelings. Yet, she found herself mute, unable to voice the words that mirrored his. The fear of exposing her heart kept her silent.

"You don't have to say it back until you're ready."

The server arrived with their meals, the interruption offering a reprieve from the pressured moment. A ribeye steak, cooked to perfection, was set before Jamal, while Carmen received her grilled chicken Caesar salad. The scent of their food filled the space between them, but the usual enjoyment was overshadowed by the weight of their conversation.

For seven long minutes, as indicated by the clock on the wall behind Jamal's head, an awkward silence hung. Carmen's gaze drifted periodically to the ticking hands, each second stretching into an eternity.

Jamal, determined to dispel the discomfort, finally broke the silence. "This steak is fantastic," he remarked, savoring a bite. The comment was simple, yet it served its purpose, offering Carmen an escape from her tangled thoughts.

"My food is good too," Carmen replied, her voice more composed than she felt. She picked at her salad, her appetite diminished by the whirlwind of emotions.

As they ate, the topic shifted to safer ground—plans for Mia's upcoming third birthday. Carmen suggested a small gathering at her home, inviting a couple of friends from daycare along with their mothers. The idea brought a smile to her face, but it quickly faded as she contemplated the space in her house.

"We can always have it at my place," Jamal offered, sensing her unease.

Carmen hesitated, weighing her pride against the practicality of his suggestion. "Are you sure? I don't want to impose."

"You know I don't mind. Besides, it'll be nice to have some noise in that big old house of mine."

Reluctantly, Carmen agreed to consider the idea. The rest of the meal passed more comfortably as they discussed party themes and potential activities for the kids.

"We'll figure it all out," Jamal said.

As Carmen watched Jamal return to his meal, her mind trailed to the words she longed to say, but didn't. In the sanctuary of her own thoughts, she finally allowed herself to acknowledge the truth. 'I love you too.' She just wasn't sure how long it would take before she was ready to say it aloud.

Chapter 21

The Courthouse

Carmen Diaz

The dark paneling of the courthouse walls made the small courtroom seem so daunting. Carmen felt her knee bouncing as she and Tony sat across from each other, facing the judge. Neither of them had a lawyer; representing themselves felt like another hurdle to overcome.

Tony had disapproved of the suggested child support amount, flooding the ensuing meeting with complaints about a "fair split." The judge listened patiently, his face void of expression .

"Your Honor," Tony whined, "I just can't afford it. $21.50 an hour, working fifty hours a week... and she makes more than me. Doesn't she have a responsibility too?"

Carmen bristled at his tone but remained composed. She unfurled a carefully prepared binder filled with receipts and financial records. "Also your honor, if I only work forty hours, I make forty-two thousand dollars a year. That would be less than he is now making," she explained. "I've been picking up extra shifts to make ends meet, which sometimes means spending more on childcare because family or friends aren't available.

The judge reviewed the evidence: Tony's pay stubs, Carmen's meticulously kept expenses, rental agreements, healthcare bills, childcare, even the price of Mia's clothes. He didn't make a sound, his gaze focused on the documents. Finally, he looked up with a serious expression .

"Mr. Lopez," he addressed Tony directly, "based on the information presented, the court is ordering $55 2.76 per month."

Tony's eyes widened in alarm. The judge's subsequent words confirmed his worst fears; Carmen had won.

The judge dismissed them with a curt nod.

"Thank you, Your Honor," Carmen smiled.

As they exited, the judge's words still echoed in everyone's thoughts. Outside, Tony stalked towards Carmen and Jamal.

He gave Carmen and Jamal a nasty look. “You should be ashamed of yourself. But instead, I see you smiling with this guy. Just remember that you are the reason our daughter doesn't have a real family.”

Jamal gritted his teeth. “You don’t have permission to lay guilt trips on her for a situation you caused. Now, if you will excuse us...” Carmen and Jamal proceeded to get in Jamal's car and leave Tony standing angrily in the parking lot.

As they drove away, Carmen let out a sigh, releasing some of the tension that had built up inside her. Jamal noticed and reached out, gently squeezing her hand in support. The gesture seemed to break down a barrier within her, and she began to open up about her past trauma with Tony.

"You have no idea what I've been through with him, Jamal," she said, her voice choked with tears. "The cheating, the constant lying, staying out late at strip clubs with his friends... and when he wasn't working, he'd just lounge around the house, playing video games all day while I was at work. I'd come home, exhausted, and still have to cook and clean for him."

Jamal was uncertain how to respond. "I'm so sorry, Carmen. You didn't deserve that. No one deserves to be treated like that."

She took a deep breath and continued. "It got to the point where I had to pawn the engagement ring he gave me to bail him out of jail. He got arrested for possession of marijuana. He has a record, and no high school diploma... it's a miracle he's working now."

"I'm so sorry, Carmen. That must have been incredibly painful for you."

Carmen nodded, her throat burning from choked back tears. "It was. And it's not just what he did. It's the emotional manipulation, the gaslighting... I felt like I was losing myself in that relationship. Like I wasn't even a person anymore."

Jamal's grip on her hand tightened. "You're an incredible person, Carmen. Don't ever let anyone make you feel otherwise. You deserve to be loved, truly loved, by someone who will support and care for you without condition."

Carmen smiled weakly, her eyes still wet with tears. "Thank you, Jamal. Just knowing that someone like you exists... it gives me hope."

Jamal couldn't believe that someone as sweet as Carmen had such an asshole like Tony as an ex-fiancé. He realized how deep her scars were and why she was afraid of love. She'd never experienced it and probably didn't even believe it could happen to her.

Carmen rummaged through her purse, searching for tissues. Her nose had began to run. Jamal merged onto the highway towards Rex.

"So, what have you decided about Mia's birthday party?" Jamal's question shifted the mood.

Carmen dabbed at her eyes. "Well, she has three friends from daycare she wants to invite." She tucked the tissue into her pocket. "Plus Lola and Felicia, of course."

"What about your parents?"

Carmen's fingers fidgeted with the zipper of her purse. "I'm leaning towards inviting them too."

"Listen, if money's tight, I can help with decorations and gifts. You know that," Jamal offered. "It's not like she'll turn three very often."

A smile broke through Carmen's face, and she let out a small laugh. "The decorations would be nice, but I want to get her gifts myself."

"My place is still available if you need more room for the party."

"Really? Then that's what I want to do."

The car slowed as they approached the daycare. Jamal pointed across the street at a discount store with bright banners in the window. "We could grab some party invitations there. That way you can give them to the teacher for those three students when we pick up Mia."

Carmen nodded. "Perfect idea."

•••••••••••

Carmen and Jamal stepped into the discount store, the cool air a welcome relief from the heat outside. The aisles were filled with colorful party supplies and trinkets.

Jamal pointed towards a section displaying balloons shaped like animals. "Mia would love those."

Carmen nodded but kept her focus on the aisle ahead. She spotted a rack filled with birthday invitations. "Over here!" she called, leading them toward the vibrant cards.

As they browsed through the selection, Carmen's eyes landed on an invitation adorned with cheerful bird and squirrel characters, both wearing party hats and surrounded by colorful confetti. The whimsical designs reminded her of that perfect day at the park when Mia laughed uncontrollably while watching the animated series that featured those same characters.

"These are cute!" Carmen exclaimed, pulling one from the rack to show Jamal.

"I think they're perfect! She really loved these guys that day at the park."

Carmen bit her lip as she studied the invitation more closely. "Mia really loves that show." She imagined Mia's smile when she saw these invitations.

"Let's make sure we get enough for everyone." Jamal said , scanning the stack for quantity.

"Definitely." Carmen began counting in her head. Three friends from daycare, plus Lola, Felicia and my parents. That was seven total. But she couldn't help but add one extra just in case someone else came to mind.

"Let's grab eight," she decided, as she collected them from the display.

They approached the register, where a teenage cashier greeted them with a smile as she scanned their items. While waiting for their total, Carmen caught Jamal glancing around at various decorations hanging from the ceiling. Bright streamers and shiny banners swayed gently above them. He had the teen to add some of those to their tab too.

"You know," he said casually, "I'm really looking forward to celebrating with you guys."

Chapter 22

3:00AM

Jamal Adams

Jamal tossed all night. Something just had him feeling uneasy. Maybe deep down, he was actually anxious about having Mia's birthday party at his house tomorrow. The fact that Carmen's parents had declined their invitation should have eased his worries, but instead, it only added to the unease that had settled in the pit of his stomach.

As he lay there, stressed, the warmth of Carmen's soft, plump ass pressed against him was too much to ignore. He knew he should let her sleep, but the temptation was overwhelming. He needed a reason to wake her at 3:00am, something that wouldn't make him seem selfish or anxious.

Jamal shook Carmen's shoulder, feigning irritation. "Hey, you were snoring," he whispered, trying to sound more tired than he actually was.

Carmen stirred, her eyes fluttering open as she rubbed the sleep from them. "I'm so sorry," she mumbled, groggily. "I didn't mean to wake you."

Jamal smiled, relieved that his ruse had worked. "It's okay," he reassured her, pulling her closer. "But since we're both awake now..." He let his words trail off, allowing the suggestion to sink in.

"Well, since we are both awake..." she echoed, her hand reaching down to trace the outline of his hardened cock through his boxers.

Jamal's breath hitched as her fingers brushed against him. He leaned in, capturing her lips in a deep, passionate kiss as their bodies melded together in the early morning darkness.

Jamal's lips pressed harder against Carmen's. The warmth of his mouth made her panties become soaked. His kiss became deeper as his fingertips traced down her torso and between her legs until two of his fingers slipped between her damp folds, eliciting a soft gasp from her as her body arched in response. Her walls squeezed him in as their tongues danced a rhythmic dance. She moaned softly from the gentle pleasure. Jamal, however, craved something more intense. He wanted to see the wild, uninhibited side of her that she kept hidden from the world.

He withdrew his fingers, leaving her wanting more. He turned on his back. "Straddle me, Carmen."

A shy smile played on Carmen's lips as she complied, positioning herself above him. Slowly, she slid down onto him, taking him in carefully. Her body adjusted to his thick girth, and she began to ride him steadily, moaning , "Ooh...yeah."

Jamal matched her rhythm, thrusting from below, "Faster!" He squeezed her ass, encouraging her to let go of her inhibitions. Carmen picked up the pace. She bounced on him, something she had never dared to do before him. He brought out a side of her that she never knew existed, and she reveled in it. Sex with Jamal was unlike anything she had ever experienced. Every stroke and grind was mind blowing, every kiss fueled her to give more. She was stepping out of her comfort zone, exploring fantasies she had only dreamed of before.

Eventually, they found themselves sitting up on the side of the bed. Jamal's hands gripped Carmen's sides tightly as she bounced up and down on him, her legs wrapped securely around his waist. Their breaths mingled, their moans heavy as their motions intensified, until they both plateaued and exploded in sync.

They shook in momentary spasms, smiling at how insanely great it was.

As the height of their orgasms subsided, they sat up on the side of the bed, still connected. Carmen's legs remained wrapped around Jamal's waist, his hands cupping her sides as they caught their breath.

For a moment, they simply sat there, basking in the afterglow of what had just transpired. Then, as if struck by the same realization at the same time, they both froze.

Carmen's eyes widened as she looked up at Jamal, her heart pounding rapidly. She hadn't moved off him. They hadn't used protection.

Jamal's expression mirrored her own. Shock and concern. He knew they should have been more careful, but in the heat of the moment, they had both let their guard down.

But even as the reality of their situation sank in, neither of them said a word. They simply held each other tighter, their arms wrapped around one another as they regained their strength.

In that moment, they both knew that even if the unplanned did happen, it would be okay. They would face whatever came their way together. With that thought in mind, they slowly disentangled themselves from each other, wiping up and settling back into bed. They cuddled close, as they drifted back to sleep.

•••••••••••

Jamal wanted to cook Mia's birthday breakfast since she and Carmen were guests at his house. "Happy birthday, Princess Mia," Jamal cheered as Carmen brought her into the kitchen to pancakes, eggs, and blueberries.

"Mal!" She ran up to him with her arms open.

He scooped her up and spun her around slowly and gently as she shouted, "Fly me...fly me Mal."

They then ate breakfast and drank orange juice as Carmen reminded Mia that her daycare buddies and Lola and Felicia, would be coming over to celebrate her turning 'the big 3.' Mia clapped her hands, and song, "Yay! Party. I have my party today."

"Yes, you will, baby girl. Happy birthday." Carmen kissed Mia on the forehead.

•••••••••••

Felicia arrived early, her mouth falling open as she stepped into Jamal's meticulously maintained home. "Wow, Jamal, your place is incredible for a bachelor pad," she exclaimed, genuinely impressed.

Jamal grinned, welcoming her with a warm handshake. "Thanks, Felicia. I like to keep things in order."

In the living room, Jamal kept Mia engrossed in cartoons while Carmen and Felicia busied themselves with decorations. Streamers in shades of blue and yellow crisscrossed the ceiling, and clusters of balloons tied to chairs and tables added a festive touch. Each balloon bore images of animated squirrels and birds, characters from Mia's favorite show.

Carmen stepped back to admire their work with her hands on her hips. "Looks great so far. Jamal, can you help hang this banner?" She held up a colorful sign that read 'Happy 3rd Birthday!' adorned with more squirrel and bird illustrations.

Jamal excused himself from Mia. "Sure thing," he said as he grabbed the step ladder and climbed up to secure the banner above the fireplace. The main-level transformed into a whimsical forest scene right out of Mia's favorite cartoon.

Meanwhile, Felicia hung character cutouts on the walls and positioned party hats adorned with tiny feathers on the dining table. The centerpiece was a large cake shaped like a tree stump, complete with icing critters peeking out from behind fondant leaves.

Carmen carefully dressed Mia in her birthday outfit. It was an adorable dress patterned with squirrels and birds. Mia twirled around before heading back to the living room. "I'm a pretty girl!" she announced proudly.

Felicia chuckled. "That you are."

Jamal knelt down to her level. "You're the star of the show today, Princess Mia."

As guests began to arrive, each carrying brightly wrapped gifts, Mia's excitement grew visibly. Takeshi, Lara, and Selena arrived with their moms eagerly greeting Mia before diving into the pile of toys Jamal had set up in one corner of the living room.

A clown arrived fifteen minutes later, livening up things more as he twisted balloons into various animal shapes. The kids gathered around him in awe as he performed magic tricks and painted their anxious faces with bright colors. The house was lit with joy as Mia and her friends played games and laughed. Every detail from the streamers to the character cutouts, contributed to an atmosphere that felt straight out of Mia's imagination. Jamal's home had been transformed into a haven of childhood wonder for her special day.

The pizza and fries arrived just as Lola stepped through the door. Jamal paid the delivery guy while Carmen helped Lola with gift bags she was carrying. Lola's eyes didn't seem to meet Carmen's though as she gestured her in. She pressed a palm against her chest and announced, "They're coming!"

Carmen and Jamal looked at one another, not knowing what to expect. Felicia heard what was going on and took the food from Jamal, then started serving the guests. Carmen and Jamal pulled Lola aside to question her about the mindset of Carmen's parents.

"Are they going to behave?" Carmen asked. "They claimed they weren't even coming."

"I don't think tío would cause trouble at Jamal's home, at Mia's party," she reasoned.

Carmen didn't seem totally convinced, but the rest of the guests were already digging into the pizza and fries, eager to finish their meals before it was time to sing happy birthday. Lola, Jamal and Carmen decided to go ahead and grab plates too, but neither of them had much of an appetite considering the anxiety they were all feeling. Carmen abandoned her plate prematurely, taking a deep breath before addressing the room. "Let's sing happy birthday," she said. Her voice was cheery despite her nerves.

Everyone gathered around Mia, singing loudly. Jamal noticed a thud of a soft knock coming from the front of the house. He opened the door to find Alejandro standing there, holding a gift box. Carmen's mother was standing behind him. Alejandro forced himself to be nice when Jamal greeted them, scrutinizing the home with a critical eye as he walked through. A part of him was impressed by the house, decorations and the care that had gone into making Mia's birthday special, but he didn't want to admit it. He was also a little envious, seeing the happiness and joy that Jamal brought to his daughter and granddaughter.

Carmen's parents walked into the decorated dining room behind Jamal, announcing "Feliz cumpleaños." to Mia. She ran and hugged them, her face lighting. Alejandro seemed to soften a bit as he saw the love and affection that surrounded his family.

For a moment, it seemed as though all of the tension and drama of the past several weeks had melted away, replaced by the simple joy of a little girl's birthday party. But as the guests began to mingle once again, Carmen couldn't help but wonder how long it would last.

Mia caught the giggles as she tore through her presents . Colorful tissue paper and ribbons littered the floor as she revealed clothes, hats, toys, books, and games. Her eyes sparkled at each gift.

After, the clown resumed his performance, pulling scarves from thin air and making coins appear behind the children's ears. The kids danced and sang along to nursery rhymes, and got their faces painted with butterflies and tigers. Mia was clearly the happiest three-year-old in the world.

The mothers gathered, chatting with Carmen about parenting and life. They nodded approvingly at how well-mannered Mia was, impressed by Carmen's dedication as a single mother.

In the kitchen, away from the festivities, Jamal overheard Alejandro speaking to Lola in hushed tones as Maria stood with them, listening in silence.

"He's better for her than Tony don't you think?" Lola asked.

"No, I don't. I don't care how fancy his house is or how much money he throws around, it won't erase the fact that he's Black and will never be fitting for my Carmen or to help raise Mia."

Jamal's nostrils flared. "Is that so? You'd rather your daughter be with someone who mistreats her because he's Hispanic than someone who's in love with her because he's Black?"

Carmen stepped into the kitchen, to refill the punch bowl she was carrying, freezing as she caught the tail end of the exchange.

Alejandro laughed coldly. "How are you any better than Tony when you sleep with my daughter out of wedlock just like he did? Neither one of you are good men. She's a fetish to you. You Black men don't like your own women because of that bad attitude *you people* got. So you come get our women."

"Every Black person I know, male or female have more class than your closed mind could ever appreciate because you're too much of a bigot to see it. Now get out of my house with this garbage! You should be ashamed of yourself on your granddaughter's birthday."

"Me ashamed? I'm the only man standing here."

Carmen's mother stood frozen, her hand pressed to her mouth, eyes wide in disbelief at Alejandro's words. She glanced between her husband and Jamal, wishing she could disappear into the floor. How had they ended up here, on Mia's special day?

Filled with rage, Jamal noticed Carmen standing in the room witnessing it all. He exhaled, hoping that she'd take the reins. "Carmen, say something to your father before I say the wrong thing. Get him out of my house."

"Jamal, it's Mia's birthday. Please. Let's ignore this just today." Carmen's voice trembled as she reached for him, desperate to keep the peace.

"Did you hear what your father said to me just now?" Jamal shot back, pulling his brows together.

Lola stood still, stunned into silence . Guests in the living room caught snippets of the confrontation over the lively music, their laughter fading as concern crept in. Whispers rippled between the mothers as they exchanged glances.

Mia, unable to see beyond the wall separating her from the chaos, whimpered softly. She sensed something was wrong.

Carmen squeezed Jamal's arm, trying to convey both apology and urgency. "I know this is wrong; I really do," she said quietly, "but please don't let him ruin today."

"Carmen..." Jamal swallowed heavily, shaking his head. "I can't do this anymore." His gaze shifted from Carmen to Alejandro before he turned away completely.

In that moment, it felt like everything unraveled for Carmen. She watched helplessly as Jamal walked out of the kitchen without another word. The finality of his footsteps echoed in her mind like a death knell.

"Wait! Jamal!" she called after him but he didn't stop.

Carmen stood there trembling as tears threatened to spill down her cheeks. She felt torn between two worlds—her father's rigid expectations and Jamal's unwavering support, and now one was slipping through her fingers.

"Mom?" Carmen looked toward her mother for support but found only embarrassment reflected in her eyes. The party continued in muted chaos around them while Felicia's and the clown's effort to keep things upbeat in the next room rang hollow against a backdrop of uncertainty and familial discord.

•••••••••••

Mia's gentle snores filled the quiet house as Jamal returned, burdened by the evening's events. He found Carmen sitting alone in the dimly lit living room, her eyes red and puffy from all the tears.

As soon as she saw him, she rushed over, her arms reaching out to hold him. "Jamal, I'm so sorry," she whispered. "I didn't want my parents to leave early. I didn't want to ruin Mia's party."

Jamal pulled away. "He disrespected me in my own home, in front of your friends and Mia's friends. And you didn't defend me. How can I be your man in the eyes of those people if you don't value me enough to stand up for me?"

Carmen's eyes welled up with tears as she tried to explain herself. "I know it looks bad, but I didn't want to cause a scene at Mia's party. I was trying to protect her from the drama."

Jamal shook his head. "You should have protected me too. You should have stood up for me."

Carmen's voice trembled as she pleaded with him. "I know, Jamal. I'm sorry. I just didn't know what to do in the moment."

"I can't do this anymore, Carmen. I can't be with someone who doesn't value me enough to defend me."

Carmen's tears spilled over, streaming down her face. "Please, Jamal. Don't do this. We can work through this."

But Jamal was already turning away. "I need some space, Carmen. I'm going to sleep in the guest room tonight."

As he walked away, Carmen collapsed onto the couch, her body wracked from the flooding tears. She knew she had let Jamal down, and the thought of losing him was unbearable.

The next morning, Carmen and Mia left Jamal's house early, without waking him up. Mia was still asleep when Carmen placed her in the booster seat. Carmen's eyes were red and swollen from crying all night, and her heart ached with the pain of their breakup.

As she drove home, she couldn't help but think about the happy moments they had shared, and the love that had once been there. But now, all she felt was emptiness and regret. The thought of being alone filled her with a deep sadness.

Jamal woke up to an empty house, the silence echoing in his ears. He knew that Carmen and Mia had left, and the thought of never seeing them again brought deep sorrow. He had given his heart to Carmen, and now it felt like it was shattered into a million pieces.

He'd never experienced this much pain, not even when Kelis broke things off.

As he walked through the house, he couldn't help but remember the happy moments they had shared, and yesterday when he and Carmen made love. But now, all he felt was heartbreak and loss. He knew that he had made the right decision, but it didn't make the pain any more bearable.

As he sat alone in the living room, he couldn't help but wonder if he would ever find love like this again. He knew that he would always carry the memory of Carmen and Mia in his heart. But for now, all he could do was try to move on, and hope that someday, the pain would fade away.

Chapter 23

Carmen's Picture

Jamal Adams

Jamal sat at his desk barely able to concentrate on analyzing Mrs. Humphrey's financial records. He pulled his phone out of his desk to check up on Keyana. He'd gotten a text from her earlier to call. When he picked it up, he saw Carmen's photo on the main screen and took a deep breath, staring at the picture of her beautiful face. Memories of him with her and Mia started flooding through his mind. He sat the phone on the desk, and put his palms over his face taking a deep breath in before sliding his hands down his face and letting it out. A bird flew into the closed window, but he didn't notice the thump.

"Why do I still have you on my screen? It's been two weeks since..." He rubbed the picture on the screen with his thumb, thinking of the last time they made love. Then, he reset his main screen with a new photo-his parents. But it didn't make him feel better now that Carmen's picture was no longer on his home screen. It just made the fact that they were over, hurt even more.

He paused a moment, and noticed the blood on his office window. His forehead crinkled with lines. Then he called Keyana, putting on a cheerful tone that really wasn't in him, but he faked it anyway.

"Hey bro!"

"Key. What's up?"

"Nothing much. Just hadn't heard from you in a minute. Plus Mom's missing you."

Jamal and Keyana chatted for a few minutes, discussing how he needed to visit their parents soon. The conversation shifted to their mother's knee, and Keyana shared her concerns about their mom overworking post-surgery.

"Mom's been working herself to the bone since the surgery. She says she can't afford not to in order to help Dad pay her medical bills, but I think it's too much for her right now."

"Mom's health should be a priority right now. Have you tried talking to her about it?"

"I have. But she just brushes it off and says she has no choice. "

"Maybe there's something I can do to help them out financially without her having to work so hard," he suggested.

"Really? What do you have in mind?"

"Well, I could offer to cover some of their expenses for a while. That way, she can cut back on hours and focus on recovering properly."

"That would be amazing, Jamal. Thank you."

"Of course, Keyana. We're family, and we look out for each other."

The conversation continued for a few more minutes as they discussed the details of their plan and how they would approach their parents about it. It was moments like these that reminded him why he chose his career path, not just for the financial stability it provided him, but also for the opportunity to make a difference in the people's lives he cared about.

"Oh, by the way, I have a boyfriend now," Keyana casually mentioned.

Jamal's eyebrows raised in surprise. "Oh, so that's the real reason you wanted to talk, huh?"

"Kinda. I haven't told Mom and Dad about him yet. I was thinking if we have a dinner with you and Carmen, me and Zin, then it will be much easier for them to handle."

"Handle? What aren't you telling me, Sis?"

Keyana hesitated before responding. "Well...he's a tattoo artist."

"Oh really? How did you meet a tattoo artist? Does he attend university with you?"

"No...I got a tat," Keyana admitted sheepishly.

"Key!" Jamal exclaimed, both surprised and concerned.

"Do they know?"

"No, it's somewhere they can't see."

Jamal shook his head. "Really? I don't want to know."

"But..."

"But, what? Is there more?"

"Yeah."

"Spill it, Key."

"Well, it's nothing bad. He's just kinda not Black. I'm in an interracial relationship too. I don't know how they're gonna take it. So, can I cook dinner and we have this double date, plus meet the parents dinner?"

Jamal was about to respond when the phone on his desk rang, sparing him from having to inform Keyana that he and Carmen had broken up two weeks ago.

"Hey Sis, got a call. I'll call you later about this."

"Okay, love you, Bro."

"Love you too, Sis."

He ended the call and answered the office line. It was Mrs. Humphrey checking up on her case.

Jamal reviewed Mrs. Humphrey's financial records over the phone, explaining the details of her profit and loss statements. "As you can see from the email I just sent, Mrs. Humphrey, your bakery has been doing quite well this quarter. Your revenue has increased by 15% compared to the previous quarter, and your expenses have remained relatively stable."

"That's wonderful news, Jamal! I've been working hard to expand my customer base and streamline my operations."

"It shows in the numbers. Keep up the great work, and I'll continue to monitor your financial records to ensure everything stays on track."

After ending the call, Jamal made his way to the breakroom, where he found Brandi Hunt eating lunch with another female accountant. The other woman had an athletic petite frame, with short, black natural curls and an attractive smile. Jamal nodded in their direction before retrieving his lunch from the fridge and heating it up in the microwave.

As he sat alone at a table, the woman whispered something to Brandi, who then approached Jamal with a confident grin. Jamal contemplated whether to brush her off or engage in conversation. He was hurt from his recent breakup with Carmen, but the prospect of a distraction was tempting. He decided to bite.

Brandi sat down across from him, casually discussing the July heat and the upcoming events downtown. As they chatted, a text reminder from Keyana popped up on Jamal's phone, asking him to confirm the dinner plans. Brandi couldn't help but notice that Carmen's photo had been replaced by one of Jamal's parents on his main screen. She had heard through office gossip about their breakup, and the change in the photo only confirmed it.

"Look, Jamal," Brandi began, sympathetic yet assertive. "I heard that you and your girlfriend broke up."

"What?" He wondered how that information had spread, realizing he had only confided in Tavaris about the breakup. He was now irritated, but he remained silent, allowing Brandi to continue.

"Someone overheard you and Tavaris talking," Brandi explained. "That doesn't matter. What matters is that you and I are both single now. You know I want you. What do you have to lose? Let's go out this weekend."

Jamal paused. He knew he was vulnerable, but the prospect of a new connection was enticing. After a moment of contemplation, he finally spoke. "What would you have in mind?"

Tavaris, always eager to provide unsolicited advice, strolled into the break room. Brandi, looked up, saw him and smiled sensing an opportunity for her to get support in her efforts to convince Jamal. "There's this cozy dance club in Decatur, doing a jazz night this Saturday. Thought it'd be fun, you know, listen to good music, drink, dance... unwind."

Tavaris nudged Jamal, smirking, "Yo, man, that's exactly what you need right now. Ms. Hunt is fire, too. Seriously smooth."

Brandi blushed at the compliments. She could tell that Jamal was considering the offer. Jamal hesitated briefly, thinking of Carmen's face. He finally answered, "All right, alright. What time?"

"Pick me up from my condo at 7:30pm Saturday." She then dug in her designer purse and pulled out a business card and a pen. She circled the cell number on the bottom of the card. Then she laid it on the table next to Jamal's phone. "Text me later, to ask for my address."

"Will do," Jamal replied, picking up the card to place in his wallet.

Brandi bounced to her feet, gathering her trash and flashing a flirtatious grin at Jamal. "Can't wait. You will not be sorry," she purred, leaning in just enough to accentuate the dip of her top.

"Da-am...Did you see those tits?" Tavaris licked his lips, rubbing his palms together as he watched her walk away.

"Yeah, couldn't help but see them," Jamal replied, unable to meet his friend's gaze.

"Man, some pussy from her is sure to help you get over the break-up blues."

"Who said I was going to hit?"

"If you don't, you are a straight fool because I'm positive she's offering up the cat?"

Jamal kept his eyes down, chewing on his lip. "Maybe it is what I need to stop thinking about Car. Because shit else is working."

Chapter 24
Comfort Zone

Jamal Adams

Jamal stood in front of the mirror with his gaze locked on his reflection. The image staring back at him felt foreign. Where was the man he had always known himself to be?

He closed his eyes tight, shaking his head slowly before opening them back up. Then he grabbed a pack of condoms from the medicine cabinet, and slipped them into his pants pocket, just incase. "This isn't who I am."

He wasn't interested in Brandi. But he needed to get Carmen off his mind. Maybe a fling or some type of friends with benefits arrangement was what he needed short term, he thought. Jamal closed the medicine cabinet back then stared at himself in the mirror, wondering who he was becoming. He'd never been the guy to engage in casual sex. He'd always been that square who respected women and didn't break hearts. But he'd recently broken Carmen's heart along with his own, and now he was considering playing with Brandi's.

Brandi wasn't the take home to mom type. But there was something about her deep down that spelled 'loyal'. She'd probably kick another woman's ass if she disrespected him, and he couldn't imagine her allowing her father to talk to him the way Alejandro Diaz did. Brandi had some good qualities, but she just wasn't right for him. So what the hell was he doing?

"Get out of your comfort zone man. Try something new."

Jamal spritzed his cologne. Then he put on the gold gradient lapel button down short-sleeve shirt hanging in his closet. As he fastened the buttons of his shirt, a dull ache struck his chest. Carmen's face flashed through his mind, her infectious smile and trusting eyes, reminding him of the life he was now walking away from. Jamal's fingers trembled slightly.

"Maybe this is what I need," he told himself, trying to convince himself as doubt started picking at his conscience. Brandi was the opposite of Carmen. She was bold, unapologetic, and seemingly immune to the kind of heartbreak he had just endured. Perhaps indulging in a casual fling was the distraction he craved, a temporary escape from the shattered pieces of his last relationship. Maybe Brandi would be okay with just a physical relationship.

Jamal's gaze drifted to the business card on the counter, Brandi's number circled in red ink. He snatched it up and punched in the digits, then texted, "*I'm on the way.*" His thumb hovered over the "send" button. The chime of a text message broke the stillness, and Jamal glanced down to see Keyana's name on the screen.

"*Bro, you good? Let me know about the double date dinner.*" the message read.

Jamal paused with his finger in mid-air. Closing his eyes, Jamal hit send. He grabbed his keys and wallet heading for the door, to pick up Brandi.

In the car, rain began to splatter against the windshield as Jamal typed Brandi's address into his GPS. The flow seemed to intensify, as he prepared his mind for the night ahead. "You're going out with Brandi. Focus on Brandi," he mumbled, maneuvering the slick streets.

As he approached her complex, coincidentally the rain abruptly stopped. He stepped out of the car, the cool damp air brushed against his face. He walked to her door and he knocked. Brandi answered. Her outfit left little to the imagination. The deep V of her top revealed quite a bit of cleavage, and the short skirt didn't seem safe for her to bend in.

"You look really beautiful," he said, the words slipping out before he could think. She smelled expensive, alluring and sexy. Almost irresistible.

"Thank you." She stepped closer with her eyes locked onto his. "You know, I've had a crush on you for the last two and a half years."

"Really? I had no idea."

Brandi chuckled, "You didn't notice me before. Hell, no one did. I didn't exactly look as put together then."

Jamal remembered the Brandi from two and a half years ago. Shyer, less confident, with an awkward shape that didn't quite fit her personality. He couldn't help but wonder if he had been the motivation behind her transformation. The thought made him uncomfortable. He preferred the gym over surgery any day.

"Well, you certainly know how to make an impression now," he said, offering her his arm. As they walked to the car, Jamal couldn't shake the feeling of unease. He had wanted a distraction, but this... this was something else entirely.

•••••••••••

The Decatur club had a lively vibe. The decor was a blend of soft lighting and rich, earthy tones that created an inviting atmosphere. Patrons lounged on plush leather couches and low-backed chairs. The speakers played smooth sounds of jazz instrumentals that blended with the laughter and chatter of the crowd. It had a classy well-dressed clientele. There were couples sharing intimate conversations, groups of friends hanging, and solo patrons lost in their thoughts over a drink.

Jamal settled into a corner booth with Brandi, who immediately waved a server over. They ordered whiskey sours and crispy calamari, along with loaded nachos topped with jalapeños and gooey cheese. The server soon returned with colorful cocktails adorned with fruit garnishes. The drinks shimmered like jewels in the dim light, brightening Jamal's mood.

As they sipped their drinks, a comedian took to the stage. He had good energy as he launched into his routine. But despite his enthusiasm, his jokes landed flat. The audience chuckled politely at punchlines that barely tickled their funny bones; they seemed more entertained by his loud polyester suit than anything he said. Jamal exchanged amused glances with Brandi as she rolled her eyes dramatically at another lackluster joke.

"You gotta give him points for trying," she murmured between sips.

"Yeah," Jamal replied, trying to stifle a laugh. "He could use some new material."

Brandi sipped her drink, admiring Jamal's appearance. "That shirt is sexy on you. But honestly? Everything looks sexy on you."

Jamal smiled as he absorbed the compliment. With every sip of whiskey and every bite of calamari, Carmen faded into the background of his mind—until recollections of her intruded once more.

"So," Brandi continued casually after noticing Jamal's momentary silence, "I'm surprised you're this hot without kids. Do you plan on ever having any?"

"With the right woman," he replied cautiously, "and after marriage."

Right then, a flashback of the last time he had been intimate with Carmen floated through his mind unbidden. They had forgotten protection and neither had mentioned it afterward. What if...

"Jamal...you didn't hear me?" Brandi's voice broke through his reverie.

"Sorry," he said quickly, shaking off the lingering thoughts. "What was that?"

"I was just asking if you came from a big family."

“I have a sister in college. And you? What was your upbringing like?”

"Growing up, it was all about family. Big Sunday dinners, everyone crammed around the table. My mom, well, she's a woman of God, but she loves to dance. My dad was a musician. He taught me how to appreciate a good groove." She paused, her gaze meeting Jamal's. "And that's what I want for myself - a big family, lots of love, someone to share it all with. You know, a good marriage, kids running around, maybe some grandkids someday."

Jamal felt guilty listening to Brandi's words. He knew she had feelings for him but as she spoke of marriage and kids all he could do was think of Carmen .

The server returned carrying his notepad.

"Ready for your main course?" he asked, glancing at their nearly-empty appetizer plates.

"Yeah, we are," Brandi replied. "We'll take another round of those." She pointed to their empty whiskey sour glasses.

"Maybe something lighter for the lady," Jamal hinted. "Something fruity, to lighten the mood."

The server jotted down their orders before retreating into the service area.

"Now this is what I'm talkin' 'bout," Brandi said, her eyes lingering on the stage.

A single spotlight illuminated a newcomer. He was a guitarist with a soulful voice and an effortless cool. His fingers stroked across the fretboard, coaxing out a sultry melody that made everyone begin to rock in their seats.

A woman in a crimson dress captured Brandi's attention. She swayed to the beat at a nearby table, moving to the music in a way that drew quite a few appreciative glances.

"Come on, Jamal," Brandi blushed, gently tugging at his arm. "Don't you wanna dance?"

He hesitated for a moment, surprised by her boldness, then let himself be pulled into the rhythm.

As they moved together, the warmth of her body pressed against him. It felt nice holding a warm body up close. She slid her arms around his neck. The alcohol was kicking in and he held her waist and pulled her closer. He felt her boobs against him. Outside of the music, the chatter of the crowd, the clinking of glasses, faded away. There was only the feeling of her arms across his shoulders, the scent of her perfume, the warmth of her body and the bassline throbbing in his chest. Jamal slid his hand further down Brandi's back, above her buttocks unconsciously. His mind drifted to Carmen briefly.

"You can squeeze it if you'd like to. I'm down for public displays of affection." Then she whispered in his ear. "The booty squeezes make me pool over." Jamal could feel his lower region respond to her words. His cock began to throb in his pants.

Brandi pressed her body closer to Jamal's. "Wow," she voiced, then giggled. Jamal felt a bit embarrassed, not wanting to come off as if his plan was to get lucky tonight, even if it had crossed his mind earlier. But a glance at Brandi confirmed she didn't seem to mind.

The server returned with their food. "Start thinking about what's on your plate. That'll help him go down," she advised. She pulled away a bit creating space between them so that he could soften up a bit. Once he'd deflated enough, they returned to their table and ate as they continued to enjoy music and conversation.

Brandi and Jamal ate and then danced a few more times. The night wore on, and eventually, Jamal drove Brandi home. Jamal pulled up in her short driveway.

"Come inside," Brandi invited, as she leaned closer to Jamal with her hand rested lightly on his thigh. "Stay the night with me."

Jamal's body responded to her touch. But his mind was telling him, *no*. He looked at Brandi, her eyes inviting, her lips slightly parted. He wanted to stay, to experience her, but something held him back, and it wasn't just Carmen.

"Brandi, I had a great time tonight," he said, fitting himself, adjusting his collar as he spoke. "But I think it's best if I head home."

"Come on, Jamal," she insisted, her hand moving up his thigh. "We had a good time. Let's not end the night just yet."

Jamal gently removed her hand, his grip firm but gentle. "I'm sorry, Brandi. I really did enjoy the evening, but I think it's best if we leave it at that."

The frustration could clearly be seen on Brandi's face, but she quickly composed herself. She leaned in, pressing her lips softly against his. "Maybe next time we can get to know each other even better," she murmured, her breath warm against his skin.

Jamal chuckled, "See you at work Monday."

Brandi smiled, flirtatiously. "See you," she replied, stepping out of the car and walking towards her condo.

Jamal watched her go. He was relieved but at the same time, his body regretted it. He started the car and pulled away, the night's events replaying in his mind. The city lights blurred past him as he drove. Despite the physical pull he felt towards Brandi, he knew he had made the right decision. For now, at least, he needed to keep things simple, to think with his big head. That wouldn't necessarily be an easy task dealing with Brandi, but he wanted to at least attempt to do the right thing.

Chapter 25
Coincidental Meeting

Carmen Diaz

Carmen waved to her older neighbor as she and Mia swung open the door to head up to the cluster box units to check her mailbox. Mia's hand clasped tightly around Carmen's fingers. She watched two rabbits eating dandelions as they approached the row of metal boxes.

Carmen opened her box. Bill, bill, late notice...and there it was. A child support payment. She opened it, revealing a check for $552.76. That would definitely come in handy every month, so why was she still feeling so overwhelmed? Carmen realized that even with that amount of money, it would still be difficult doing everything on her own. Being a single person, period, was expensive in this economy.

Carmen massaged her temple; that annoying headache from earlier was still there. She woke up with it, and decided to call in this morning. She knew it was due to not getting enough rest. Even though it had been weeks since the breakup, she had stayed up late crying, thinking about Jamal.

As they headed back to their tiny house, a guy who lived around the corner was heading toward the box units, checking her out and grinning. He was definitely hot, but she was still longing for Jamal. In fact, she was surprised the guy even looked her way wearing an oversized tee, with no makeup, a stress zit on her cheekbone, and a messy ponytail on hair that needed the roots touched up weeks ago. But it wasn't just Carmen that missed Jamal. Mia constantly asked when he was coming back over to play with her stuffed rabbits.

Carmen and Mia went back inside their house to grab her purse and keys. "Let's get ready to put this check in the bank and fill up my tank. We'll get you a milkshake or smoothie on the way home, okay?"

Mia's eyes lit up with excitement. "Yay! That's great, Mama!"

So, they got in the car and headed to the bank. Carmen thought about how supportive Jamal had been by going to court with her that morning for the child support hearing. He'd always been there for her. She wanted to kick herself for failing him with her dad, allowing him to be publicly emasculated. Maybe she never deserved his love.

As they pulled into the bank's parking lot, Carmen couldn't help but feel a flood of guilt pour over her. She had been so focused on her own struggles that she had let Jamal down when he needed her the most. She knew she had to make it up to him somehow, but she wasn't sure how. He didn't want to speak to her. He'd made it clear that he wanted distance, and he hadn't made any attempts to reach out.

Mia's excited chatter brought Carmen back to the present. "Mama, can I have a strawberry milkshake?"

"Of course, sweetie," Carmen replied, forcing a smile. "Strawberry it is."

As they walked into the bank, Carmen couldn't let go of the feeling that she had to take action to reconcile with Jamal. She just hoped it wasn't too late.

The line at the bank was moving at a snail's pace, and the clerk seemed to be in a foul mood. He huffed and puffed as he processed each transaction, making it clear that he didn't want to be there. Carmen tried to remain patient, but it was difficult with Mia getting antsy.

Finally, it was their turn. Carmen handed the check to the clerk, who barely looked up as he processed it. "Is there anything else?" he asked gruffly.

"No, that's all," Carmen replied, trying not to sound annoyed.

The clerk handed her the receipt and turned his attention to the next customer. Carmen rolled her eyes as she and Mia exited the bank.

As they walked to the car, Carmen tried to decide which credit card to use for the gas and milkshakes. She didn't want to use her debit card if she could avoid it. She pulled out a Visa and swiped it at the pump, but it was declined. "Ugh," she muttered, digging through her purse for another card.

Mia looked up at her with concern. "You okay, Mama?"

"Yes, I'm fine, mija," Carmen reassured her, finally finding a card that worked.

As she unscrewed the gas cap and pumped, she noticed a man watching her from across the parking lot. He was tall and athletic, with a muscular build that made one assume that he worked out regularly. His skin was a rich mahogany, and he kept his hair short and well-groomed. The man was in his early thirties, dressed casually in fitted jeans and a designer t-shirt and expensive sneakers.

"Hey, are you Carmen Diaz?" he hollered out with an odd smile on his face.

Carmen's heart began to race. She had no idea who this man was, and her first thought was that he was going to kidnap her and Mia and take their organs. She reached for her pepper spray, but before she could grab it, the man approached her.

Carmen hesitated for a moment before responding. "Yes, that's me," she replied quickly returning the gas nozzle to the pump and screwing her gas cap back on.

"I'm Jamal's friend Tavaris. I've seen pictures, and he told me about you." He had taken the day off for a dentist appointment.

Carmen's heartbeat slowed down as she realized who he was. "Oh, right. I've heard about you too. You're his best friend." She would have never guessed who he was by the way he was dressed—no shirt and tie, just casual clothes.

They chatted for a while, and Tavaris asked how she was doing following the breakup. Carmen lied and said she was okay.

"How's Jamal doing?"

Tavaris hesitated for a moment before responding. "He's...seeing someone else."

"He's seeing someone else?"

"Well, they're dating. They've gone out a few times."

Carmen tried to hide her disappointment, but it was clear that she was upset. Tavaris apologized for bringing it up and promised to let Jamal know that he had run into her.

As they said their goodbyes, Carmen couldn't help but feel like she had lost someone who was not just important, but irreplaceable. She had always known that Jamal was a catch, but she had hoped that they would have a chance to work things out. Now, it seemed like that chance was slipping away.

Carmen got back in the car and dialed Jamal's number for the first time in weeks. The phone rang three times before going to voicemail. She wanted to cry, but instead, she took a deep breath and texted him. "*I need to see you today. I need to tell you something.*"

Jamal had seen her number on the caller ID and had decided not to answer. But when he read her text, he worried. He wondered that she may be pregnant since they didn't use protection the last time they'd been together. So he texted her back, telling her that he was at the office completing some work he was behind on and that she could come over in about two hours. She replied, "*Okay. I'll be there.*"

Carmen then remembered Mia. She quickly called Felicia to see if she could watch her. "I know it's a drive and little notice, but..."

"I get it girl," Felicia said. "This may be your last chance, especially if he's seeing someone."

Carmen drove to Mickey Burgers and ordered two strawberry shakes and a chicken nugget meal for Mia. When she got home, she quickly freshened up, dressed in a casual skirt outfit, and hot curled her hair while she waited for Felicia to arrive to watch Mia.

Carmen's outfit was a floral print skirt that fell just above her knees, paired with a simple white blouse. She wore a pair of strappy sandals that showed off her freshly painted toes. Her long, bleach blonde hair cascaded down her back in spirals, framing her face and highlighting her deep brown eyes.

When Felicia arrived, Carmen thanked her and hurried out to the J.S. Barnes & Associates building where Jamal worked. She was a bit shaky as she walked into the lobby. She started counting in her head, trying to calm her nerves. She rode the elevator up to the third floor and made her way to Jamal's office.

As she approached his door, she could hear him talking on the phone. She hesitated for a moment before knocking softly. Jamal looked up and saw her standing there. He quickly ended his call and gestured for her to come in.

"Hey," he said, his voice sounding distant and guarded.

"Hey," Carmen replied, her voice shaking slightly. "I'm sorry I bothered you while you were working, but I needed to talk to you."

Jamal nodded, gesturing for her to take a seat. "What's going on?" he asked, his eyes searching hers for any hint of what she was about to say.

Carmen took a deep breath and began to speak, her words tumbling out in a rush. "I just wanted to tell you that I'm sorry for everything that happened. I know I hurt you, and I never meant to. I was just scared and confused, and I didn't know how to handle everything."

Jamal listened quietly, his expression unreadable. When she finished speaking, he leaned back in his chair and sighed. "I appreciate you coming here and telling me that, Carmen. But I'm not sure where we go from here."

Carmen panicked as she realized that he may not be willing to forgive her. She tried to calm her voice. "I understand if you don't want to be with me anymore. But I just wanted you to know that I still care about you, and I'm willing to do whatever it takes to make things right between us."

Jamal looked at her for a long moment, his eyes searching hers. Finally, he spoke. "I care about you too, Carmen. But I need some time to think about everything. Can we talk again in a few days?"

Carmen nodded, trying to hold back her tears. "Okay," she said softly. "I understand."

As she stood up to leave, Jamal walked over to her and gave her a hug. "Thank you for coming here and telling me how you feel," he said, his voice gentle.

Carmen hugged him back, trying to memorize the feel of his arms around her. She knew that she may have lost him for good, but at least she had told him how she felt. She took a deep breath and walked out of his office, trying to hold her head high. But then she paused, turning back around.

Carmen stepped into Jamal's office. She closed the door behind her and took a calming breath before speaking. "Jamal, I need to tell you something. I was wrong for not standing up to my dad that day at Mia's party. I should have said something. I was weak and I was wrong. There's no excuse. I was just torn. But...I choose you Jamal."

Jamal looked at her with a hard stare. "You choose me now? Why?"

Carmen took a step towards him. "I haven't spoken to my parents since that day. It's as if I lost them and you, all because I couldn't bear to speak to them after they caused me to lose you. Jamal...I won't let you go. I can't lose you. I love you!"

Jamal's eyes widened in surprise. He had waited for those words since he told her that day at the restaurant when they had lunch together. He couldn't ignore her words because he could see in her eyes that they were sincere. "Carmen...I—"

"Jamal, I choose you. If my family can't accept you, they can't be a part of my life. I won't lose you." She walked over to him and gazed deeply into his chestnut eyes. He rubbed a stray spiral from her face, brushing his hand across her cheek. His lips drew to her rosy lip gloss. He kissed her softly, then more intensely. Before they knew what was happening, they were removing clothing and grinding each other on the client chair that sat in front of his cluttered desk. It was a lucky thing that he'd forgotten to open his blinds that morning.

As they kissed, Jamal's hands roamed over Carmen's half naked body, exploring every curve and contour. She moaned softly as he caressed her breasts, her nipples hardening under his touch. He trailed kisses down her neck, his tongue darting out to taste her skin. She arched her back, pressing herself closer to him.

Jamal gently lifted her and then set her down on a clear area of his desk. He kissed her deeply, his hands exploring her body. She wrapped her legs around his waist, pulling him closer. He could feel her heat radiating through her skirt, and he knew that she wanted him just as much as he wanted her.

He slid her skirt up, revealing her lacy panties. He leaned over and kissed her thighs, his tongue tracing patterns on her skin. She moaned softly, her hands tangled in his hair. He hooked his fingers under her panties and slid them off, tossing them aside.

Jamal swooped Carmen into his arms and laid her on the small leather couch in the corner of his office. He entered her slowly, moaning at the feeling of her warm juicy walls caressing him. She gasped as he filled her completely, her body trembling with pleasure. He began to move, his thrusts slow but hitting the right spots. She met him stroke for stroke, her hips rising to meet his.

Their bodies moved together in perfect harmony, their breaths mingling as they kissed. After they had been at it intensely for several minutes, Jamal could feel his climax building, and he knew that he wouldn't be able to hold out much longer. He quickened his pace, going deeper.

Carmen cried out as she reached her climax, her body shuddering as she came. Jamal followed soon after, his own release overwhelming him. They lay there for a moment, their bodies entwined, their breathing ragged.

As they caught their breath, Jamal looked into Carmen's eyes. "I love you," he whispered.

"I love you too," she replied, her voice filled with emotion.

Carmen and Jamal cleaned up with a box of wet wipes he had on his file cabinet. They dressed quickly, chuckling about what had just happened. Jamal walked Carmen to the door, his hand resting on the small of her back. "I'll call you later," he said, still slightly out of breath.

"Okay," she replied, her eyes shining with happiness.

As she walked out of the office, Jamal felt a sense of contentment. He had finally won the heart of the woman he loved, and he knew that nothing would ever come between them again.

Chapter 26

Out of Your Mind

Jamal Adams

Jamal drove to his parents' house from the jewelry store, talking to Tavaris on his cellphone as he steered down the dim road.

"You did what, bro? Are you out of your mind?" Tavaris's voice crackled through the phone.

"Nawl man, she's who I want to be with. Besides... even though her father said some real racist shit that day, he said something that was true."

"And what was that?"

"If I keep sleeping with Carmen without marrying her, how am I treating her any better than Tony did?"

"Man, are you freakin' serious?" Tavaris burst into laughter. "I can't with you, Jamal. I'm just hoping you'll snap out of this. It's like she put some type of spell on you. Man, you didn't eat any spaghetti she cooked lately, did you?"

"Stop it man, no. I want to do the right thing by her. She's the one. I've never felt this way for anyone."

"What about Kelis?" Tavaris reminded.

"Kelis was never serious about us. That entire relationship was one sided. This time, it's reciprocal."

A short silence fell, and Jamal felt good knowing Tavaris understood his genuine love for Carmen.

Then Tavaris finally replied, "Negro, you should have at least done a test run with Brandi before buying a ring. Can't believe you let her go to get back with this chick and all her problems."

"Man, I've told you a million times—if you think Brandi's all that, then shoot your shot."

"I might have to now," Tavaris laughed. "I was trying to give you a chance, but you didn't do right. At least this Carmen chick is kinda fine. She had that red ass zit on her cheek the day I saw her at the gas station, but she's naturally cute."

"T, you're a straight fool." Jamal chuckled despite himself. "But you're my homeboy. Talk to you later. I'm pulling up at my parents'."

"Good luck telling them about this."

"Yeah... need more than luck," he replied grimly. "Say a prayer for me man. Seriously."

"Gotcha bro. Let me know how it goes." The line clicked off.

Jamal took a deep breath as he parked outside his parents' house. He unfastened the top button of his shirt and pulled out the small velvet box from the jewelry store bag resting on the passenger seat. He glanced down at it before sliding it into his right pocket.

Jamal walked up the driveway and knocked on his parents' door. Keyana answered, rolling her eyes.

"You never got back to me regarding the double date. What's up with that?" Keyana crossed her arms tightly over her chest.

"Sorry, Key... there was just a lot going on with me and Carmen at the time. I really didn't want to get into it. I mean, to be honest, we were on a break when you approached me with that."

Keyana's brows shot up. "Things are working out between you guys now though, I hope?"

Jamal reached into his right pocket, pulling out the small velvet box. He opened it slowly to reveal an impressive diamond ring.

"Whoa! Is this what I think it is?" Keyana gasped.

"If you think I'm asking Carmen to be my wife, then yes."

"Wha-what did you just say?" Jamal's father shuttered as he walked into the living room.

Jamal faced his father. Millard's brow furrowed deeply in disbelief.

"Married? You promised us you wouldn't," Patrice stopped mid-stride, as she walked into the room behind Millard.

"Mom," Jamal began, feeling the tension coil around him like a vice. "You said I wouldn't. But none of that matters now. Carmen and I love each other and I want to make her my wife."

“Have you lost your mind?” Millard’s voice rose slightly. “She has a kid, a deadbeat baby daddy—”

“—and bigots for parents,” Patrice finished for him, shaking her head in disbelief.

Jamal placed a hand to his temple. His parents only knew the watered-down version of the situation but still disapproved. They weren't even aware of what happened at Mia's birthday party.

"Dad, I didn't come to get your permission. I came to check up on you guys and announce what I was going to do."

Millard shook his head. "We're fine," Patrice lied, trying to hide the pain in her eyes from being on her recovering knee too long at work. She shifted on her knee, trying to relieve the discomfort .

"That's good." Jamal smiled at them, determined to lighten the mood. "I have something that'll make you feel even better." He reached into his wallet and pulled out two gift cards—$600 for Kruegs Groceries and $250 for Chepron Gas Station.

"What is this all about, son?" Millard had mixed feelings. He was grateful, yet with him being the provider, it felt odd with Jamal gifting so much money.

"Dad, it's just a little gift for Mom. Keyana helped nurse her back to health after surgery, so I wanted to do something too."

Millard nodded appreciatively as Patrice pulled Jamal in a tight embrace. "Thank you," she murmured against him. “This means so much.”

"It's a beautiful ring," she added after pulling back slightly. "I'm sure she'll love it!" A playful elbow nudged Millard's side as he softened under his wife's gaze.

Millard cleared his throat. "Son, if that’s who you want... then I give my blessing too."

Just then, Jamal's phone buzzed against his leg. Carmen's name lit up the screen.

"Hey," he answered, unable to keep the excitement from spilling into his tone. "I'm actually on my way over."

Jamal slipped the engagement ring back into his pocket as he wrapped up his visit with his family. The air felt lighter now; he had shared a piece of himself with them, and their support meant a lot. Keyana walked Jamal back to the front door.

"Maybe I should wait before telling them about Zin," Keyana suggested, glancing up at him with a teasing smile.

"One shock at a time is best," Jamal chuckled back. "I want to meet him first. How about that?"

"Sure thing." Keyana smiled, closing the door behind him.

Jamal was super excited as he made his way to the car. He thought of Carmen and wondered how she'd react to his proposal. He just hoped she'd say yes.

•••••••••••

Carmen smoothed the material of her pink sleeveless dress, pleased with how it flattered her shape. She felt both beautiful and a bit confused, wondering why Jamal had insisted on a last-minute outing when she had planned a cozy evening at home.

"Why did you have me get dressed last minute to go out?" she asked, glancing sideways at him. "I told you I'd cooked. At least Mia was already at Tony's mom's house."

Jamal shrugged with an easy smile as he steered the car into the parking lot of the restaurant. "You had a babysitter. I wanted you to enjoy a Friday out. That's all."

Carmen turned her gaze to the restaurant's entrance, noticing the warm glow spilling from inside.

"How are things with Tony?"

"Oh my..." Carmen giggled. "It seems as if he has calmed down tremendously since the child support payments started. He's not popping up anymore or calling. I don't think we'll have to worry about him disrespecting our relationship anymore. I think he's being forced to grow up through this."

"That's good. I'm glad."

They stepped out of the car, and Jamal walked around to open Carmen's door before offering her his hand.

"Wow," she said as they approached the entrance, taking in the elegant ambiance that filled the four-star Italian restaurant. "No wonder you wanted me to put on something nice."

"Kinda fancy here," he remarked with a grin. "At least I have a gorgeous woman on my arm to match the vibe."

"Well, thank you," she smiled. "You don't look too shabby yourself Mr. Adams."

Carmen's eyes were equally pleased by Jamal's appearance, lingering on the fresh fade that sharpened his features and made him appear even more handsome than usual, if that were even possible. The tailored midnight-black suit against his espresso complexion was a total showstopper. Then there was his pearly whites, those expressive eyes, and the gleam of that sexy full beard. They all contributed to her temperature rising. To Carmen, he looked dangerously handsome, although she wanted to believe he wasn't aware of the effect he had. She felt a thrill, both excited and nervous, and realized she'd never felt this way with anyone else.

As they entered the Renaissance styled wrought iron doors, a subtle scent of garlic and herbs hit them. A pretty brown-skinned hostess with coily bangs and a high-bun showed them to their table. Jamal held Carmen's chair for her as she settled in at their table, and she couldn't help but feel special under his attentive gaze.

“Nice place,” she said, glancing around at the soft lighting and tasteful decor.

“Yeah,” Jamal replied, leaning back slightly as he scanned their surroundings. “So, how's work?”

" Mr. Hancock's been so annoying lately! Always hovering over my shoulder like I don’t know how to count pills."

"What about you?" Carmen asked, sipping her water. "Anything interesting happen today?"

Jamal chuckled, dabbing his mouth with his napkin. "Actually, I met Mr. Johnson's wife today."

Carmen raised an eyebrow in surprise. "Really? What's she like?"

"She's the sweetest," Jamal said, smiling fondly at the thought. "They came in to discuss adjusting their budget further. Apparently, they want to save up for a big anniversary trip next year."

"Oh my gosh! That's so romantic! How long have they been married?"

"Twenty-five years," Jamal replied proudly on their behalf. "Can you believe it? They still act like newly-weds when they're together, despite all of Johnson's complaining about her math skills."

"That's adorable! It's nice to know that true love does exist."

Just then, their server approached, ready to take their order for wine and appetizers before they delved into entrees.

While they waited for their drinks and food to arrive, soft Italian instrumentals played softly in the background over their conversation.

As Carmen spoke animatedly about how well Mia was doing at daycare, her eyes lit up with excitement. Jamal couldn't help but steal glances at her lips and collarbone exposed by the neckline of her dress; something about it felt mesmerizing amidst their casual chatter. She was undeniably beautiful.

The appetizers and wine soon arrived, the clinking of glasses melding with the soft melodies drifting from the speakers. Carmen relished the first sip, letting the rich flavors consume her palate as she glanced across the table at Jamal. He looked relaxed, his smile genuine as he gestured animatedly while sharing a story about his latest encounter with a particularly stubborn client.

They went ahead and ordered their main courses, their conversation flowing easily as they enjoyed their wine. Jamal leaned forward, curiosity sparking in his eyes as he switched up the topic of the conversation a bit.

“So, do you enjoy being a pharmacy technician?” he asked, tilting his head slightly.

Carmen considered his question for a moment, chewing a mouthful of bruschetta . “It’s rewarding in some ways,” she admitted. “I love helping people feel better, but it can be tedious. Sometimes I wish I had pursued something more... dynamic.”

“Like what?” he pressed gently. "In five years, where would you want to be?"

“I’ve always dreamed of starting my own health and wellness business one day,” she replied, her eyes lighting up at the thought. “In five years? I want to be doing something that makes me excited to wake up every morning.”

Jamal took mental notes as he listened intently. "And what about kids? You ever think about having more?"

Carmen hesitated briefly before answering. "Definitely. If I could afford it, I'd love to send my kids to a Christian private school. Growing up Protestant had so much beauty and so many values were instilled early on."

Jamal felt an instant connection with her upbringing as he shared similar beliefs rooted in Baptist traditions.

"I love that idea," he said with sincerity. "I think meaningful education is important for them."

Carmen smiled as they delved deeper into dreams of family life.

The server returned then, clearing away their appetizer plates and setting down steaming entrees that carried enticing aromas throughout the air.

"Bon appétit!" he chimed cheerfully before slipping away again.

As they began to eat, Jamal's attention drifted toward his phone. He excused himself for a moment, leaving Carmen alone with her thoughts and half-finished meal.

In his absence, Carmen pulled out her phone and texted Felicia. She sent a few pictures of the restaurant and her plate as well. A few seconds later, Felicia's response popped up:

"Looks yummy, Sis. Let that man spoil you! Have fun."

Carmen smiled at the screen.

Jamal soon returned with a suspicious smile plastered across his face.

"Everything okay?" Carmen asked.

"Everything is beautiful." He leaned closer, locking his gaze with hers. Something about him looked so good tonight, and Carmen felt a flutter within her that mirrored the glow in Jamal's expressive eyes.

They finished their meal, savoring each bite until their plates sat empty, with the exception of a few crumbs. Dessert soon followed; Carmen felt stuffed but couldn't help the smile that spread across her face, as if she could hold much more joy in her stomach.

The server approached with two dessert plates covered by elegant black dome covers, accompanied by a violinist gliding behind him, the strings whispering a gentle tune that filled the air with romance.

With a flourish, the waiter set down the plates before them and stepped back. Jamal glanced at Carmen, then lifted her dome cover with a slow dramatic flair.

Carmen was in shock as she caught sight of what lay beneath—the small velvet ring box nestled on the plate.

Time seemed to halt as Jamal dropped to one knee beside her. Her eyes widened and misty tears welled up as she instinctively covered her mouth with trembling hands.

“Carmen Aurora Diaz,” he began, his voice steady yet soft. “Will you make me the happiest man in the southeast and be my wife?”

A hush fell over the restaurant as all eyes turned toward them, anticipation crackling like static electricity. The world around them faded into nothingness.

"Yes! Yes, a million times yes!" The words burst forth from Carmen’s lips before she even realized it. Joy radiated through her body like fireworks igniting on New Year’s Eve.

Jamal slipped the ring onto her finger with shaking hands as they both stood up, wrapping each other in an embrace that felt like coming home after years of wandering.

Applause erupted from every corner of the restaurant, cheers mixing with laughter and joy as they hugged tightly and shared sweet kisses.

The singer took this moment to launch into a romantic ballad while they continued to embrace. Each note floated through the air, weaving seamlessly into their celebration. It was the most beautiful moment Carmen could have ever dreamed of.

Chapter 27

Satin and Lace

Carmen Diaz

Lola and Carmen stood in the bridal shop in downtown Newnan, surrounded by a sea of satin and lace. The sales lady was a petite woman with a gap-toothed grin. She spoke one trillion words per hour as she presented Carmen with yet another wedding dress.

After nearly seven try-ons, Carmen finally found the perfect dress - a stunning Liza Morgan design with a fitted bodice and a flowing, strapless-skirt. Her eyes lit up as she gazed at her reflection in the mirror. Lola, resplendent in a bright yellow sundress, stood behind her with a big smile.

The only problem was, the matching veil had a tear. "I can offer you 30% off on the veil. Or, we do have separates over here."

The saleswoman led them to a section in the corner, where a rack of random veils sat next to a rack of less eye-catching dresses. Carmen and Lola began to search through the veil rack, trying to find something that matched the dress. Lola carefully lifted a veil, examined it, and then hung it back up. Carmen scrutinized each veil, but wasn't impressed with any of them.

"None of these work. Can you order it?"

"Unfortunately, not. We are discontinuing this style here. Perhaps you can try this dress shop, they carry Liza Morgan designs."

She handed Carmen a card, which read "Bride's Paradise, Augusta". Carmen couldn't conceive the thought of driving so far for a veil. There had to be another solution. She turned to Lola, who was still rummaging through the veil rack.

Just then, Lola shouted. "Check this out!" She held up a veil with the same pattern, but a slightly different cut. Carmen took a look at it and smiled. Then she tried it on. She loved the way it fit. It was perfect! She charged the dress and the veil on the debit card of the account Jamal recently added her to.

Carmen couldn't believe how everything seemed to be falling into place. She and Jamal already had the location figured out - a chapel downtown. They were allowed to invite up to 15 guests and add some of their own personal touches for $2500. This even included 10 wedding photos up against their decorative background walls. Felicia knew a girl at her job who designed cakes. The only thing left was a dress for Mia (flower girl), Felicia and Keyana (bridesmaids) and Lola, maid of honor.

Carmen only met Jamal's family briefly after the proposal, and didn't know Keyana well, but she still felt it would be a great idea to make her a bridesmaid. She was thinking about ordering their dresses online. Whatever she was going to do, it needed to be done soon. The big day was right around the corner.

Lola stood beside Carmen at the register, admiring the veil that perfectly complemented the intricate lace detailing on her wedding gown, as the sales woman placed it in the hanging bag. "You looked stunning in that dress and veil, Car. Jamal's not gonna know what hit him when he sees you walking down that aisle."

"I can't believe this is all really happening. It feels like a dream."

"It's not a dream, it's your reality. You and Jamal are meant to be. I'm so happy for you, prima."

"Thank you, Lola. I don't know what I'd do without you." She pulled her cousin into a tight hug, grateful for the unwavering support in all this, even though it went against what Carmen's parents felt .

As Carmen and Lola left the bridal shop, Carmen announced to Lola that she was ready to tell her parents about the wedding. "Are you sure? Why even involve them and get your head all messed up before your big day? You know they're not coming and they won't give their blessing either." Lola shook her head, but instead of driving Carmen back home, she drove to Carmen's parents' house.

As they pulled up in front of the house, Carmen took a deep breath and prepared herself for what was to come. She knew her parents would be disappointed, but she hoped they could at least be happy for her.

"You can do this," Lola whispered as they got out of the car.

Carmen knocked on the door and waited nervously for her mother or father to answer. Maria opened the door. Her father, Alejandro, stood behind her. Both of them looked surprised to see Carmen there with Lola. "What brings you here?" Maria asked puzzled.

Carmen took a step inside and closed the door behind her. "I have something important to tell you both." She hesitated for a moment before continuing.

She could see the surprise spew over her parents' faces, especially Alejandro's. His initial thought was that she had come to announce a breakup. A smile crept across his lips as he waited for the inevitable words, "I should have listened."

But Carmen didn't give him that satisfaction.

"Jamal and I are getting married."

Maria's face fell as she processed the news. Alejandro looked equally shocked but said nothing. Carmen could see the disappointment in their eyes, but she pressed on anyway. "We're planning a small ceremony in Newnan next month," she said, holding up a hand to forestall any objections. "It's just going to be us and a few close friends."

Maria opened her mouth to speak but closed it again without saying anything. She looked at Carmen with a mix of sadness and resignation. "I guess we should be happy for you," she finally said in a small voice.

Carmen could see that this wasn't going to be an easy conversation as she looked at both her parent's expressions, but she was determined to stand up for herself and Jamal. She took another deep breath before continuing, "I know you both disagree with our relationship, but this is what I want ." She paused for a moment before adding softly, "I guess, I just want to have your blessing."

Carmen looked directly at her father. Alejandro's earlier smile had totally vanished.

"I want you to walk me down the aisle."

Alejandro clutched his chest as if struck by a physical blow. "Are you out of your mind! There is no way I'd walk you down the aisle to marry that guy. How can you bring disgrace to your family like this?"

Lola exchanged glances with Maria, who stood frozen in disbelief. Both sensed the storm brewing between her husband and daughter.

Carmen's eyes filled with tears, but she held firm against her father's wrath.

"Listen to me—"

"He's not a good man," Alejandro cut her off. "You're making a fool of yourself."

Lola finally stepped forward, refusing to let Carmen face this alone. "He is really a good guy, tío. He treats Mia as if she's his own. When Carmen needs help, he gives her money for her bills. He's the main reason she was able to make it on her own after leaving Tony. Tony wouldn't even let her take the bed or sofa to sleep on. She slept on an air mattress. The Latino guy isn't better for her."

Alejandro's face reddened as he listened to Lola's words but refused to accept them. "You're wrong! " he snapped back at Lola.

Maria looked from daughter to husband, caught in the middle of an emotional tug-of-war.

“Carmen,” Alejandro said firmly, “If you say 'I do' to this Jamal guy, be prepared to never set foot in this house again. From that day on out, I will no longer have a daughter.”

The finality of his statement stifled any hope Carmen had for understanding or reconciliation. She felt as if she'd been struck by lightning; an invisible force threatened to tear apart everything she believed about family loyalty and love.

"Carmen..." Maria said finally as Carmen felt tears prickling at the corners of her eyes.

Maria's hand clutched her mouth tight, tears pouring down her cheeks like heavy rain. Carmen's eyes bulged in her father's direction. She wanted to cry, but she was frozen by his words. Lola grabbed her gently by the arm. "Come on, Car. Let me take you home."

Carmen numbly allowed herself to be led out of the house and into Lola's car. The engine roared to life, but inside the vehicle, sound was hushed.

As they drove, Carmen stared out of the window, replaying her father's ultimatum over and over. Alejandro's harsh words echoed in her ears, shattering the remnants of her childhood memories and everything she believed about her relationship with her father. The father who had loved her with all his heart as she grew up was now disowning her. It was an unbearable agony that was making it hard to breathe.

Lola glanced at Carmen from time to time, her own heart aching for her cousin's pain. "I'm so sorry, Carmen. You know you did the right thing by telling them."

Carmen didn't respond; she couldn't find the words. She felt like a part of her had been ripped away, leaving a gaping wound that might never heal. Her eyes turned toward the passenger window as she silently allowed suppressed tears to stream from her eyes.

Buildings and people passed by in a blur of colors and shapes. Magnolia trees swayed gently in the breeze, children played in front yards, and couples strolled hand in hand. It all seemed so surreal now, as if she were watching a movie from behind a glass wall.

"You're not alone in this," Lola said softly.

Carmen was grateful for Lola's presence even though words felt inadequate to express it. The weight of what had just transpired was too overwhelming; she knew she had to learn to live past the pain, to live without her parents in her life.

When they finally pulled up in front of Carmen's tiny home, Lola turned off the engine but made no move to get out. Instead, she looked at Carmen .

"Remember why you're doing this. You deserve happiness with Jamal and Mia deserves stability."

Carmen wiped away the last of her tears and took a deep breath. "Thank you," she whispered, finally finding her voice again.

Carmen hugged Lola, stepped out of the car and walked toward her house. Each step felt heavy but for now, though, she had to focus on moving forward and building the life she envisioned with Jamal and Mia.

Chapter 28

A Lap Dance

Jamal Adams

Jamal sat at his folks' dining room table with his parents and Keyana eating fried chicken, sweet corn bread, coleslaw and green beans. Jamal's dad, Millard, looked as if he were lost in thought as he chewed a mouth full of beans. "I suppose it wouldn't hurt to ask Tisha about Nathan being the ring bearer. It's been a while since we've seen them." Nathan was Tisha's son, who was Jamal's cousin. His cousin on his father's side. Tisha wasn't the easiest person to get along with. She always had to have things her way and she copped an attitude when she couldn't.

Keyana's phone buzzed again, drawing everyone's attention. She glanced at the screen and quickly typed a response before placing it face down on the table. Jamal couldn't help but smirk, knowing full well that it was Zin, Keyana's secret boyfriend.

Jamal's mom, Patrice, raised an eyebrow at Keyana. "You know, you really should put that phone away during family dinners. It's not polite."

Keyana sighed, rolling her eyes. "I know, Mom. I'm sorry. It's just— "

"Zin?" Patrice asked, finishing Keyana's sentence. Jamal seemed surprised that Keyana had obviously told their parents about her boyfriend. "Seems like he can be a little needy sometimes, all that texting."

"Well, that's what happens when you start dating a drop out with tattoos and a motorcycle. You never know what you're gonna get," Millard shook his head.

Keyana shot her dad a glare. "That's not fair, Dad. Zin is a good guy. He's just...different from the guys I usually date."

"That's true, Key. But it's important to remember that family is always there for you, no matter what. And we just want what's best for you."

"I know, Mom. And I appreciate it. But, Zin is a good guy." Keyana grabbed her glass of tea. She always had a tendency to drink excessively at the table when subjected to awkward conversation.

Jamal cleared his throat, bringing the conversation back to the wedding. "So, about Nathan. Do you think he'd be up for it? I know Tisha can be a handful, but I think it would mean a lot to her if Nathan was a part of the wedding."

Millard nodded. "I'll give her a call tomorrow and see what she says. It couldn't hurt to ask."

Patrice clapped her hands together, a smile spreading across her face. "Oh, that would be wonderful! I can't wait to see little Nathan again. He's such a sweet boy."

"Just remember, Patrice, he's not so little anymore. He's eight years old now," Millard reminded, grabbing another chicken wing from his plate.

"Oh, he'll always be my little grand-nephew. I can't wait to see him in a little tuxedo, carrying the rings down the aisle."

Millard took a last mouthful of slaw. "So, what's the deal with Carmen's family? They ain't coming to the wedding?"

Jamal hesitated, tightening his grip around his glass of tea. "Carmen's parents... They refuse to come."

Patrice clucked her tongue, shaking her head. "I couldn't imagine not coming to my child's wedding. It's just not right."

"Bigotry will make you do some crazy things." Millard drank a swig of his tea. "Son, just know that this marriage won't necessarily always be easy. Even though Carmen will be your wife, she'll always have a bond with her parents and will always desire their approval whether she admits it or not. Once y'all have kids, things will likely get even tougher with all this. Just be prepared son, that's all. Not trying to discourage you."

The table fell silent. Jamal fixed his gaze on his plate.

"Well, I'm excited about Carmen asking me to be a bridesmaid. She seems cool. I like her," Keyana blurted feeling the need to cheer up her older brother after their dad's gloomy speech.

Jamal looked up, smiling slightly, "She likes you too, Key."

"My dress is arriving tomorrow. I can't wait to try it on!"

"Just make sure it's appropriate, Keyana. You don't want to be falling out of your dress at the wedding," Patrice interjected.

"Mom, please. I know how to dress myself."

Jamal, sensing an impending argument, suggested, "Why don't you ask Zin to come with you, Key? That way you two can dance at the reception together, and we get an opportunity to meet him."

"Yeah, that sounds like a good idea."

After dinner, Jamal stood up, stretching. "Alright, I'm heading out. Tavaris rented a space for my bachelor party."

Millard raised an eyebrow. "You sure about this, son? You know how these things can get wild."

Jamal chuckled, "I'm sure, Dad. It'll be fine. Carmen's supportive, and she's going out with her friends to celebrate too." Jamal hadn't necessarily wanted a bachelor's party, but Tavaris insisted it was a must.

••••••••••••

As Jamal drove to the venue he thought about his dad's warning. But, he wanted to have faith that he and Carmen could get through anything. He couldn't help but smile thinking of Carmen's beautiful face and long blonde hair. The city lights blurred past him, as he drove deep in thought.

The venue Tavaris had rented was a spacious loft apartment in a trendy part of downtown Atlanta. Exposed brick walls met polished concrete floors, creating an industrial-chic vibe. A massive, worn Persian rug lay in the center of the main seating area, partially covered by a low glass coffee table littered with poker chips and playing cards. A large flat-screen TV mounted on the wall played a basketball game on mute. A well-worn pool table occupied a corner, its green felt surface illuminated by a hanging pendant lamp. A bar area, complete with stools and a mirrored backsplash, offered an array of liquors and mixers. Oddly, sheer, lavender curtains draped the large windows, an unexpected touch in the otherwise masculine space. Scattered throughout the room were bunches of metallic, heart-shaped balloons tied to furniture and light fixtures, their surfaces reflecting the ambient light. A faint scent of vanilla warred with the aroma of expensive whiskey.

Jamal greeted his old college buddies, their laughter echoing in the spacious loft. He hadn't seen most of them in years, the demands of adult life and careers scattering them across the country. Catching up over a game of pool, Jamal reminisced about their shared college escapades, the years melting away as they traded stories and playful jabs.

Maurice lined up his shot, his brow furrowed in concentration. "So, Jamal, how's the accounting gig treating you? I heard you're making big moves at the firm."

Jamal grinned, chalking his cue. "It's going well, man. I'm up for a promotion soon. It's been a lot of hard work, but it's paying off. How about you? Last I heard, you were killing it in the marketing world."

"Yeah, it's been a wild ride," Maurice replied, sinking his shot. "I'm heading up a new campaign for a big client. The hours are crazy, but I love the challenge."

Terrence, who had been quietly sipping his beer, chimed in. "That's great, guys. I'm still plugging away at my startup. It's been a rollercoaster, but we just landed a big investor."

Jamal clapped Terrence on the back. "That's awesome, Terrence. I always knew you'd make it big with that entrepreneurial spirit of yours."

As Jamal lined up his next shot, Maurice's curiosity got the better of him. "So, J, you're tying the knot. Who's the lucky lady?"

A soft smile played on Jamal's lips as he thought of Carmen. "Her name's Carmen. She's amazing, man. Beautiful, smart, and she's got a heart of gold."

Terrence raised his eyebrows, impressed. "Sounds like you hit the jackpot, Jamal."

"Yeah. I can't wait to make Carmen my wife," Jamal beamed a wide smile. "What about you guys? Any special women in your lives?"

Maurice shrugged with a sly grin. "I'm still playing the field, you know me. But I've got my eye on this girl at work. She's a firecracker."

Terrence, on the other hand, blushed slightly. "Actually, I've been seeing someone for a few months now. Her name's Lisa, and she's incredible. She's been so supportive of my startup dreams."

Jamal raised his beer in a toast. "To the women in our lives, whether they're our future wives or our future prospects. May they keep us on our toes and in our hearts."

The three friends clinked their bottles together, the bond of their friendship as strong as ever despite the years and distance between them.

Ten minutes into their reunion, the catering service arrived with mountains of barbecue ribs, smoked chicken, and all the fixings. The aroma filled the loft, making their stomachs rumble in anticipation. As they piled their plates high, a knock echoed through the space. Tavaris peered through the lavender curtains, a mischievous glint in his eyes. He turned to Jamal, a smirk playing on his lips. "Looks like we have a visitor. Why don't you get the door, man?"

Jamal, eyebrows raised in curiosity, set down his pool cue and headed towards the entrance. He swung the door open to reveal a gorgeous honey-brown toned woman, dressed in a lavender satin robe, its silky fabric clinging to her curves. Before he could react, she dove into a seductive dance, her body moving, gyrating to the pulsating hip-hop beat someone turned up in the back of the loft. She wrapped a sheer lavender scarf around his neck, her movements were both artful and provocative. Entering behind her were at least eight more women of a variety of hues, all similarly attired, followed by two men dressed in sharp suits. The men immediately peeled off to the side, engaging Tavaris in a hushed conversation about the services being rendered. Meanwhile, the women dispersed throughout the loft, laughing and chattering. The suited men directed the placement of a portable stripper pole in the center of the room. Once the pole was secure, they announced a set of rules for interacting with the dancers, before taking up positions in the corners of the room, where they stood guard.

The strippers captivated the room with their mesmerizing group and solo performances. Some showcased their skills on the pole while others danced seductively on the floor. They were all hot. At least 3 had huge boobs. But they all had large, perky butts. Each woman possessed a unique allure, from their voluptuous curves to their confident movements. Jamal couldn't help but blush as the stripper he had opened the door for focused her attention on him, her eyes locked on his as she swayed to the music.

She walked over to him after her performance and leaned in close, her breath warm against his ear. "She must be mighty special to land a cutie like you." She brushed the back of her hand against his cheek. Jamal felt a shiver run down his spine at her touch.

"She is," Jamal replied, a smile tugging at the corners of his lips. "Carmen's one of a kind."

The stripper grinned, her fingers trailing down his chest that was exposed through his partially buttoned shirt. "Well, lucky her. And lucky you, getting to experience all this before you tie the knot."

Jamal chuckled nervously as his eyes darted around the room. He noticed Tavaris and a few of his old college buddies watching the exchange, amused.

"Man, you're about to be glued to one woman the rest of your life," one of them called out, raising his beer in a toast. "Live a little!"

Jamal frowned slightly, not appreciating the way they made marriage sound like a prison sentence. Being with Carmen was anything but a trap; it was a blessing he couldn't wait to embrace.

The stripper sensed his hesitation and leaned in closer making her voice lower and more seductive. "How about a lap dance, handsome? One last thrill before you say 'I do'?"

Jamal hesitated, but he felt the peer pressure and the woman in front of him was definitely alluring. "Alright, why not?"

His buddies erupted in cheers as the stripper began to dance, her body moving in perfect sync with the pulsing beat of the music. She circled his lap, her hips swaying hypnotically as she ground against him. She was definitely skilled in her techniques. Jamal's breath caught in his throat, his hands instinctively gripping her waist as he lost himself in the moment, picturing her with absolutely nothing on. It took willpower to control his thoughts, but he couldn't control his body.

"Wow," the stripper whispered, her lips brushing against his ear. "Feels like someone's enjoying himself."

Jamal blushed deeper, suddenly aware of his body's reaction to her skilled movements. He tried to focus on controlling his mind, but with her voluptuous body pressed against him and the music thumping in his ears, it was a losing battle.

A few of the fellows in the background continued to watch and cheer them on. The remaining guys danced with the other strippers. You could hear their laughter echoing through the loft. It was a whole vibe. The catered barbecue was devoured with gusto, the ribs and chicken disappearing quickly. Drinks flowed freely, fueling the celebratory mood. Between dances, Jamal and his friends continued to catch up, reminiscing about their shared past and discussing their present lives as well as the party. The night was a potent cocktail of nostalgia, good food, strong drinks, and alluring entertainment. Jamal felt genuine appreciation for Tavaris. He knew he'd put a lot of thought and effort into planning the bachelor party, and it had exceeded all expectations.

As the party wound down and the last of the guests stumbled out, Jamal pulled Tavaris aside. "Thanks, man. This was exactly what I needed. You're a true friend."

"Anytime, bro," Tavaris replied, clapping him on the back. "Wouldn't miss it for the world. And hey, thanks for choosing me as your best man. Means a lot."

"I could thank you even more," Jamal said, reaching into his pocket. "I think you'd make use of this." He held out a small, lavender card, stained with a smudge of barbecue sauce.

"I peeped her slipping it into your pants pocket during that lap dance." Tavaris burst out laughing, snatching the card.

"Man, you saw that?

"She was fine, wasn't she?"

Jamal chuckled. "She was alright," he admitted, having flash backs of the feel of her body against his. "So," he continued, changing the subject, "what about Brandi? You still pursuing that?"

"Already on that," Tavaris replied, a bit overly confident.

Jamal's eyes bulged. "Real talk?"

"No cap. First date is next Wednesday night. Soul food and rhythm and blues at some club in Doraville."

"All the way in Doraville?"

"It's worth it," Tavaris said elbowing Jamal. "Especially if she puts out the first night."

"Man, you're a trip," Jamal chuckled. "But I love you, man."

He pulled Tavaris into a brief, brotherly hug. They locked up the loft, stepping out into the cool night air, each heading home.

Chapter 29
A Good Man

Carmen Diaz

Pastor Holmes was nice enough to marry Carmen and Jamal at a discount, even though he hadn't seen Jamal there at his church in years. He was Jamal's childhood pastor. The old church had gone bankrupt, and Pastor Holmes went through a bout of depression after and decided just to perform marriage ceremonies and counseling thereafter. He had a rental space where he offered these services. There was a chapel there, a photo room for wedding pictures, an office where the pastor counseled, and two dressing rooms for the bride and groom.

Carmen sat at the vanity mirror with mascara trails marking paths down her cheeks. Her white gown hung perfectly on her naturally toned frame, but her face couldn't hold a smile.

"I just wanted them here. Even after everything."

Felicia dabbed at Carmen's face with a tissue while Lola rummaged through her makeup bag. The small dressing room felt even smaller with the despairing atmosphere.

"Here, drink this." Felicia pressed a cold water bottle into Carmen's trembling hands. "Deep breaths, girl."

"What kind of wedding doesn't have the bride's parents?"

"The kind where the bride is strong enough to choose love over everything else." Felicia's eyes met Carmen's in the mirror. "Think about Jamal waiting out there. Think about the man who loves you and Mia more than anything."

The mention of Jamal's name brought a fresh wave of tears. "He deserves better than this mess."

"Stop that right now. He deserves exactly what he chose - you. And you deserve him."

Carmen wiped her eyes and gazed at her bare face in the mirror. Through the tears and smeared makeup, she saw something else - the woman Jamal fell in love with. The mother who'd do anything for her daughter. The fighter who'd chosen happiness over obligation.

"God really did answer my prayers, didn't He?" Carmen smiled weakly in the mirror.

"That's right." Felicia squeezed her shoulders. "He sent you a good man who loves you right."

"And now we just need to fix this makeup before that good man sees you looking like a raccoon." Lola joked, drawing a genuine laugh from Carmen.

As Felicia's skilled hands worked to restore Carmen's makeup, Lola stepped away to a quiet corner, to secretly text Carmen's parents. The message was simple but urgent: "*Please come. Your daughter needs you today more than ever.*" Alejandro texted back within seconds with a reply that Lola wasn't willing to accept.

"I forgot something important at the house. I'll be right back." Lola's heels clicked against the floor as she headed for the door.

"But—" Carmen's eyes widened in panic.

"Trust me, I'll make it back in time." Lola's tone left no room for argument.

A knock at the door brought Keyana's bright face peeking in right after Lola left out. "That was Tavaris at the door. He says my brother's pacing in the groom's dressing room. He's ready for his bride."

This news only made Carmen worry more about whether Lola would return on time. But she and the other ladies continued to get ready, hoping Lola would return soon, as promised. The bridesmaids' teal dresses played beautifully against both Felicia and Keyana's skin tones, the chiffon fabric flowed like water with every step they made. When Lola finally rushed back in ten minutes late, she slipped into her maid of honor dress. It was a slightly darker shade of teal with delicate beading across the bodice that set it apart from the others.

"Sorry, sorry!" Lola scrambled to get ready, swishing as she moved.

Felicia put the finishing touches on Carmen's makeup, then stepped back to admire her work. "Remember, don't be nervous. This is the day you've been waiting for." She blew Carmen a kiss and smiled.

• • • • • • • • • • • •

Keyana and Felicia glided down the aisle in their teal chiffon dresses as the sun streamed through the chapel's stained glass windows like a spotlight. Felicia's goddess braids were swept into an elegant updo, while Keyana's hair was in a sophisticated high bun. White and teal hydrangeas adorned the end of each pew, their petals echoing the bridesmaids' dresses.

Moments later, Lola followed as the maid of honor, her gown a slightly deeper shade of teal, set apart by delicate beading across the bodice that caught the light with every step. Her wavy chestnut hair cascaded over one shoulder in loose curls, and a satisfied smile curved her lips as she walked proud, composed, and quietly glowing.

The intimate chapel sparkled with white tulle and twinkling lights woven through crystal-draped archways. Tavaris stood tall in his black tuxedo with a teal pocket square, while Jamal's parents sat in the front row. His mother was in a silver beaded gown, his father in a classic black suit. Zin had cleaned up surprisingly well in a dark suit, though his tattoos peeked from beneath his sleeves. Jamal's cousin Tisha wore a purple wrap dress, her locs styled in an intricate crown.

Nathan strutted down the aisle with the rings, his little tuxedo pristine and his locs pulled back neatly into a low ponytail. Tisha's eyes darted around the room, gauging reactions to her son's performance. Tavaris smiled at Jamal, genuinely happy for him.

Mia toddled down next, sprinkling rose petals from her little basket. Her white dress had a teal sash, and she wore tiny flowers in her dark curls. The guests couldn't help but collectively sigh at how adorable she was.

As Luther Vandross' strong vocals filled the chapel with 'Here and Now', Carmen's hand trembled on the door handle of the dressing room. When she opened it, her heart stopped! There stood her father in his tuxedo. His eyes were glistening with unshed tears. Through her own suppressed tears, she noticed her mother slipping into a back pew, wearing a traditional Mexican dress in deep blue.

Carmen's white strapless skirt-gown hugged her curves before flowing into a modest train. Her bleached blonde hair was styled in loose waves beneath her veil. As her father took her arm, joy, relief and love overwhelmed her. This was everything she'd wanted - her parents' blessing, the man of her dreams waiting at the altar... Each step down the aisle brought her closer to the future she'd chosen, one filled with love rather than obligation.

The closer Carmen came, all Jamal could see was her, the woman who'd turned his life upside down without even meaning to. He was struck by her breathtaking radiance, a beauty that went deeper than the surface, and his heart filled with a love that felt solid, certain, and hard-won. In that moment, he no longer saw the struggles or the timing that once tried to keep them apart. There was just the woman who chose to let him love her and the forever he had been ready for all along.

Pastor Holmes stood before them. His presence was a comforting reminder of Jamal's childhood faith. He began the ceremony with a warm smile, his voice carrying through the chapel.

"Dearly beloved, we are gathered here today to witness the joining of Jamal Adams and Carmen Diaz in holy matrimony. Marriage is a sacred bond, a promise of love and commitment that endures through all of life's joys and challenges."

The pastor turned to Jamal, who stood tall and proud, his eyes never leaving Carmen's face. "Jamal, do you take Carmen to be your lawfully wedded wife? Do you promise to love, honor, and cherish her, in sickness and in health, for richer or poorer, forsaking all others, as long as you both shall live?"

Jamal's voice was strong and clear. "I do."

Pastor Holmes then addressed Carmen, who radiated joy despite the tears glistening in her eyes. "Carmen, do you take Jamal to be your lawfully wedded husband? Do you promise to love, honor, and cherish him, in sickness and in health, for richer or poorer, forsaking all others, as long as you both shall live?"

Carmen's voice trembled with emotion, but her words were resolute. "I do."

The couple exchanged rings, the simple bands symbolizing their eternal love and commitment. As they slipped the rings onto each other's fingers, their hands trembled with anticipation and joy.

"By the power vested in me by the state of Georgia, I now pronounce you husband and wife. Jamal, you may kiss your bride."

Jamal pulled Carmen close, his hands cupping her face with tender reverence. As their lips met in a passionate kiss, everyone erupted into cheers and applause. Tears of happiness streamed down Carmen's face as she melted into her husband's embrace.

Alejandro watched his daughter with pride and bittersweet joy. Though he had struggled to accept her choices, seeing her so radiant and in love softened his heart. Carmen's mother dabbed at her eyes with a handkerchief, overcome with emotion at witnessing her daughter's happiness.

Felicia and Lola cheered loudest of all, their faces beaming with joy for their best friend. Keyana wiped away a tear, her heart full of love for her brother and new sister-in-law. Tavaris grinned from ear to ear, knowing that his best friend had found his perfect match. And though Jamal's parents felt uneasy about this union in the beginning, they could clearly see that Jamal and his new wife had something special.

As Jamal and Carmen turned to face their guests, hand in hand, the love and support that surrounded them was clear to see. They had chosen each other, and in doing so, they had chosen a future filled with love, laughter, and endless possibilities.

Chapter 30

Epilogue

Carmen Diaz

It was a beautiful Saturday. The sunlight was bright streaming through the bay windows of the house as Carmen and Keyana huddled over a stack of bridal magazines spread across the coffee table. They were debating color schemes.

"Emerald green would look stunning with your complexion, Key." Carmen pointed to a bouquet arrangement.

Through the sliding glass doors, squeals of laughter erupted as Mia, now a lanky eight-year-old, spun her pink hula hoop alongside her longtime buddies Takeshi and Lara.

Heavy footsteps thundered down the stairs, followed by high-pitched giggles. Jamal emerged with Jamal Jr. sitting up on his broad shoulders. JJ's hands were gripping his father's ears.

"We gonna make sandwiches!" JJ announced. He was a perfect combination of both his parents. He was a caramel complexion with thick 3c curls. Overall his face looked like Jamal's but his deep brown eyes were identical to Carmen's.

"Tuna again?" Carmen raised an eyebrow at her husband.

"What can I say? Like father, like son." JJ's favorite lunch was tuna sandwiches and Cheetos. Jamal's grin matched JJ's as they disappeared into the kitchen.

Keyana twisted her engagement ring. It was a delicate silver band with a black diamond, perfectly matching Zin's aesthetic. "Who would've thought I'd end up with a tattoo artist?"

"Who would've thought he'd turn out to be such a good man?" Carmen smiled, remembering their initial reservations about Zin. After Keyana informed everyone that she and Zin were dating, a lot of other things came out that no one was aware of, including the fact that he had two baby mamas and one was best friends with his sister. Despite his complicated past with his children's mothers, he'd proven himself dedicated to Keyana and his thriving business.

The peaceful afternoon was refreshing, considering the tumultuous early days of Carmen and Jamal's relationship. Tony's absence had become just another fact of life, his child support payments were the only reminder of his connection to Mia.

JJ's voice rang out from the kitchen, "Daddy, more mayo!"

"That's enough mayo, little man. We want to taste the tuna too."

Mia came hopping inside with Lara and Takeshi. "Mama, look!" she exclaimed, pointing at the bleeding scrape on her knee.

Carmen knelt to inspect the injury. "What happened, baby?"

"I tried a cartwheel and landed funny."

"You guys were really testing your skills out there today," Carmen said leading them to the kitchen sink. She reached underneath the lower cabinet for the first-aid kit, then gently cleaned the wound before applying a bandage. "But next time, be more careful, okay?"

Mia nodded, distracted by the promise of lunch. Carmen had Mia and her friends to wash their hands. Just then, Carmen's phone buzzed with an incoming call from Lola. "Hey, Car!" Lola's voice crackled through the speaker. "Guess what? Felicia got a new car. It's gorgeous! But you won't believe what that troublemaker at work did this time..."

Carmen listened for a moment, her eyes on Mia and her friends as they dried their hands and bounded towards the dining table. "Lola, can we talk later? Lunch is ready." This was the same woman who had been causing trouble at Lola's job for the past 10 years. Why they hadn't gotten rid of her by now, Carmen couldn't figure out.

"Sure thing. Talk soon!" Lola replied before hanging up.

Carmen joined everyone at the table, where Jamal and JJ were already setting out plates of tuna salad sandwiches and bowls of Cheetos. Everyone dug in.

"Mama, there's a boy at school who eats boogers," Mia announced between bites, her friends nodding in agreement.

"Mia!" Carmen chided gently. "That's not something we talk about during meals."

Keyana chuckled at her niece's innocence. "Kids are so cute."

"Keyana, you and Zin will have a family just like this in a few years," Jamal responded.

Keyana smiled, glancing at her engagement ring. "I hope so."

"How's Tavaris' baby doing?" she asked Jamal after a moment.

"The baby is well." You could tell there was trouble in paradise just from his tone. Tavaris' relationship with Brandi was anything but stable these days. Tavaris still craved his freedom while Brandi sought commitment.

Carmen smiled with some positive news. "My parents said they were free to babysit JJ and Mia next Saturday, so you can go ahead and buy those tickets for the play."

Jamal was excited at the prospect of a date night with his beautiful wife. Keyana continued to eat, watching the kids and picturing her own future children.

Carmen drifted into her own deep thoughts, reflecting on how far her relationship with her parents had come. They had given Jamal a hard time in the beginning because he was Black. But, over time, they had grown to love Jamal and his family, accepting them wholeheartedly. It meant the world to Carmen and Jamal that her parents loved both JJ and Mia equally, never treating JJ differently for being biracial.

Their life together was beautiful, almost perfect. The only sadness that lingered was the fact that Tony had deserted Mia, but his absence only served to highlight his true character. Jamal was a blessing though stepping up, being a wonderful stepfather to Mia and showing her the love and support she deserved.

As Carmen watched her family, she realized that this love was everything she had ever wanted in a relationship and more than she could have ever dreamed of. She couldn't believe there was a time when she had been *on the fence* about taking a chance on loving Jamal. Sometimes you must take a chance, or you'll risk the opportunity of losing something truly great.

THE END

•••••••••••

If you were drawn to the emotional journey in *Love on the Fence*, continue the ride with *Perfect Love*. In this gripping story of marriage, betrayal, and devastating choices, Avery and Marcell Phillips must confront the secrets, temptations, and tragedies threatening to tear their seemingly perfect life apart. Follow me on Amazon to stay connected with future releases and emotionally powerful stories about love, secrets, and the consequences of the choices we make.

Click here to download Perfect Love: https://www.amazon.com/Perfect-Love-Psychological-Fiction-Shattered-ebook/dp/B0FRYHPQYG?ref_=ast_author_mpb

NEXT BOOK: IN THE SPINOFF SERIES

Brandi Hunt is chasing stability and a ring, while Tavaris Johnson is convinced love doesn't need paperwork or lifelong monogamy to be real. When he suggests moving in instead of proposing and a flirty string of text from a neighbor sends Brandi spiraling, things get messy fast (even though Tavaris hasn't actually cheated). Add the fact that they're both accountants at the same office, and now the tension isn't just at home—it's spilling straight into the workplace.

ABOUT THE AUTHOR

Queenink Watkins, a Georgia native, began her author career as a children's author in 2015, publishing her first title under her real name (Schertevear Q. Watkins). She has also assisted countless other authors in their writing journey through her publishing company (Baobab Publishing) which provides services to indie authors.

As far as adult fiction goes, Queenink writes stories that blend emotionally complex themes with suspense, romance, family drama, urban grit, and small-town charm. Her work often features strong, relatable women, facing personal battles, set in working-class and middle-class communities. Whether it's love triangles, infidelity, or deep emotional bonds tested by betrayal and redemption, her stories are driven by complicated relationships and powerful character arcs.

JOIN MY EMAIL LIST

SCAN THE BARCODE TO JOIN

Scan the barcode to join my email list to obtain biweekly book recs of authors I read and those I rock with as well as sneak peeks and release info for my upcoming projects. I want to get to know you!

FOLLOW MY TIKTOK

www.ingramcontent.com/pod-product-compliance
Lightning Source LLC
LaVergne TN
LVHW091030080826
845145LV00002B/424

* 9 7 8 1 9 4 7 0 4 5 4 9 1 *